Man of the Match

In the moonlight she saw a glint in his eye. "A skinny dipping party?"

She was confused for a moment, then she realised that he could only see her shoulders. Unaware that she was wearing a strapless bikini he possibly thought she was swimming naked. She was desperately embarrassed, and hoped that the darkness hid her reaction.

"No, I'm wearing a bikini."

He raised his eyebrows, and then she was startled to feel his hands suddenly circling her waist. In the sea her skin felt hyper sensitive, and his touch was like an electric shock.

He felt up her side to where her bikini top was. "So you are."

And there she was, almost in the arms of a complete stranger who had been extremely rude to her only a few hours earlier.

Forbidden Lessons

"This is something that could ruin both our lives."

When 18-year-old Laura first sees her new German teacher her world is turned upside down. She can't get Mr Rydell out of her mind. Is it coincidence that she keeps bumping into him outside class or does he share her feelings? He's totally forbidden fruit. But the two of them are soon risking everything for passion.

Every rule is broken... who will be forced to pay the price?

Set in the UK in the 1980s, "Forbidden Lessons" is based on a true story.

Summer's Edge

He's fighting it but he needs this as much as I do.

When Stewart Walker finds out the girl he kissed is a student at his school he's furious and determined to keep away. But 18-year-old Alice has fallen hard and won't give up. She wants him to teach her body and her mind, even though a relationship is strictly against the rules. He's struggling to resist the attraction despite knowing he could lose his job.

Throughout the illegal raves and festivals of Britain's summer of '92, Alice and Stewart dance closer and closer to the edge.

Available in paperback or eBook from Lulu.com

MAN OF THE MATCH

by

Noël Cades

First Printing, 2015

ISBN: 0992501741
ISBN-13: 978-0-9925017-4-7

To Audrey Truscott

I dream of lands where summer smiles,
And soft winds blow from spicy isles,
But scarce would Ceylon's breath of flowers be sweet,
Could I not feel thy soil, New England, at my feet!

Poems of Nature: The Last Walk in Autumn
John Greenleaf Whittier

1. Tropical Escape

Lying on the beach, warmed by the tropical sun under the dappled shade of a palm tree, the grey misery of London seemed very far away. The sand was soft under her skin, the sky azure above, and a whole week of golden days and balmy nights stretched before her.

It was heartbreak that had impelled Cara to book a last minute holiday to Sri Lanka. She hadn't even thought or cared about where she went, she just wanted to get away. At twenty-one, after Declan's betrayal, she thought her whole life and happiness were over.

As a student she didn't have a lot of money to spend on her trip. After turning down a few cheap Spanish resorts for fear of being surrounded by couples and too many people in general, she'd found a last minute deal to Sri Lanka at an amazing price. A cancellation holiday, the travel agent had told her. Being sold for a fraction of the price because she had to travel the very next day.

Cara took it. She had no one to leave and nothing to lose. Anymore, anyway. A week in the sun would burn away her misery and leave her re-energised and ready to face the world again.

Here, on this island paradise, she didn't want to think about Declan. But the hurt and the betrayal haunted her. He said he had been happy for them to wait until marriage, so why had he indulged in the brassy charms of his secretary Lucinda? Cara felt so stupid, so humiliated. Declan had obviously planned for her to be the sweet and innocent little wife, while he privately enjoyed a string of mistresses.

Suddenly her thoughts were interrupted by an unwelcome shower of sand. It was flung all over her, sticking to the sun oil on her body.

Furious, she sat up and saw the culprit. A red cricket ball had landed on the beach next to her, clearly with some force given the amount of sand it had thrown up.

Just as she looked around to find out who had thrown it, a man came running towards her with a cricket bat in his hand.

"Yours, I take it?" she said, her annoyance clear in the coolness of her tone.

He scowled instead of apologising. "This is a private beach. There wasn't supposed to be anyone else on here."

Eclipsed against the sun, Cara saw that he was tall, rugged and very bronzed. There was something familiar about him, though she was sure they'd never met.

In the distance she saw several other men, clearly in the progress of playing beach cricket. They hadn't been there when she had arrived and settled herself at the far end of the beach.

"The hotel concierge directed me here," she told him.

"You're staying at the Pavilion?" When she nodded he looked even more annoyed. "My apologies for disturbing your sunbathing." He sounded anything but sorry.

"It's quite alright, I was due for a swim," she said.

His eyes flicked over her body in its bikini, far skimpier than she usually wore because it wasn't summer holiday season in England and there hadn't been much choice in the shops.

Cara felt herself flush and hoped her growing tan would hide it.

For a moment he lingered. She thought he was about to say something else so she waited.

But he turned abruptly and left her. His lack of farewell left her even more infuriated. What a rude man, she thought.

She waited until he had strode down the beach back to the other players before she rose to get in the water. If the ball came her way again, she would throw it into the sea and let him swim for it.

Dining alone didn't bother Cara. She enjoyed her solitude and she had brought a tonne of study notes with her. Her last year of university was turning out to be a rigorous one and she wanted to be prepared for the final terms.

She sat by herself on the veranda, surrounded by lush tropical plants, with some books spread out on the table as she enjoyed a pre-dinner cocktail.

Once again, her peace was disturbed.

"Your boyfriend neglecting you?"

The speaker was a man with a round, friendly face. Cara recognised him as one of a group of sporty looking men who had arrived together - rather late and looking the worse for wear - for breakfast that morning. He was with a couple of them now.

She realised he was fishing to find out whether she was here with a boyfriend or not. Inventing one might be a useful safeguard against future approaches, but then she might be forced to produce one later in the week.

"I'm actually here on a study trip."

One of the others turned over one of her books, Principles of Biochemistry.

"Hardly holiday reading, is it?" he said. "All work and no play. We're having a party tonight, why don't you come?"

Cara tried to decline but they were all insistent, teasing her by reading out quotes from her textbooks, so eventually she laughed and agreed. One party wouldn't hurt, and she could just drop in for a single drink and leave early. "Where is it?"

"Just here, at the hotel. In the front bar."

They were all heading into the town for dinner first and couldn't persuade her to join them there. Finally they left, and Cara was free to go to the hotel dining room alone as planned.

* * *

Cara had gone to her room after dinner as the party apparently didn't start until a bit later and she didn't want to be the first one there. She changed into a white sundress and some strappy heels. Her sun-kissed skin didn't need much make-up. The dark circles she'd had under her eyes from weeks of crying herself to sleep had also faded. She had slept much better here, away from it all and all the memories of Declan.

Her hair fell in dark, glossy waves that framed her face. Not bad for a newly-avowed nun, she thought. If only she was of a religious mind she could have gone into a convent and never had to see another man again. But she knew that wasn't her vocation, even if she was determined to avoid the male sex for the foreseeable future.

Downstairs the party was already in full swing so she needn't have worried about arriving early. The whole bar had been taken over and there was loud music and much merriment.

"We wondered where you'd got to." It was the round-faced young man and his friends. "Have a drink."

A glass was put into her hand and she was led through the crowd, some of whom were already dancing to the music, to where the bar opened onto another veranda where more people were milling around.

Introductions were made, and as she was chatting to Jeremy - as her new friend turned out to be called - she looked up to see a face across the crowd practically glaring at her.

It was the tall, surly man from the beach.

Despite the mutual dislike Cara felt she also noticed how good looking he was in a rugged, very masculine way. She tried to tell herself that most men look better in a clean shirt, with a good tan, but she had to admit that he looked better than most.

But he had made his rudeness clear, so she didn't acknowledge him but turned her attentions back to Jeremy.

Yet something drew her thoughts towards the other side of the room like a magnet. She had to force herself not to look over in his direction, and to concentrate on what the people around her were saying. Perhaps it was because he reminded her of someone, and her thoughts wouldn't rest until she had figured out who.

The merriment grew with the night and the alcohol, and someone suggested going for a midnight swim. There was huge enthusiasm for this among the young men there.

"You'll come, won't you?" one of them urged her.

12

Cara was wearing a bikini underneath her sundress, as being strapless it didn't show under the dress. She supposed she could go for a swim, it did seem like a lovely idea.

There was a full moon shining down on the waters, it was still the start of her holiday, and the sea was warm and calm under the stars.

Cara was dimly aware that she had probably drunk more than she meant to, but right now she didn't care. A group of them entered the water first with others following. Shallow and sandy, it was quite safe even in the dark.

There were the usual splashing games and riotous behaviour. People diving under the water and grabbing one another's legs and pulling them under. Someone found a beach ball and attempted a game of water polo.

The ball was thrown to Cara and she reached up for it but someone else grabbed it, and she fell against a third person instead.

"I'm sorry."

As she turned she was mortified. It was the man from the beach.

"Good to see you," he said. Was he being sarcastic? His tone sounded quite polite and formal.

Cara didn't know what to say. "I wasn't expecting it to turn into a swimming party."

In the moonlight she saw a glint in his eye. "A skinny dipping party?"

She was confused for a moment, then she realised that he could only see her shoulders. Unaware that she was wearing a strapless bikini he possibly thought she was swimming naked. She was desperately embarrassed, and hoped that the darkness hid her reaction.

"No, I'm wearing a bikini."

He raised his eyebrows, and then she was startled to feel his hands suddenly circling her waist. In the sea her skin felt hyper sensitive, and his touch was like an electric shock.

He felt up her side to where her bikini top was. "So you are."

And there she was, almost in the arms of a complete stranger who had been extremely rude to her only a few hours earlier.

She couldn't take her eyes off him.

He was gazing right back at her. There was an intense look in his eyes that seared her.

Suddenly he leant closer to her and his lips were on hers. His mouth was hard but tender. He tasted of salt and his tongue was warm as it slid alongside hers and entwined with it.

His hands gripped her more firmly around the waist, not letting her go.

Cara's mind was in a whirl. What was she doing? Every ounce of sense ought to have seen her push him away and flee, but her body sang with desire for him.

She noted the sculpted muscle of his neck and shoulders, the darkness of his wet hair, close cropped at the nape of his neck. He was much more of a man than any boyfriend she had dated before. He was also much older, perhaps ten years older than her, she thought.

His hand supported the small of her back as his mouth left hers and travelled across her cheek and down her neck. He was tasting her, devouring her.

Waves lifted them up and down, and Cara felt incredible physical closeness to him as they clung together. They could have been one body.

I don't even know his name, she thought.

As if he read her mind, he broke off at one point and looked her, his eyes burning with the physical desire he felt for her.

"I'm Matt," he said.

"Cara."

She could hardly speak, her voice seemed like a whisper carried away by the waves.

"Cara mia." And he kissed her again.

Nothing had ever felt so right in her body and so wrong in her head.

2. A new day

Matt Curran was furious with himself when he woke, his head splitting, the next morning. At the age of thirty-two and as England cricket captain he was supposed to behave more responsibly than trying to drunkenly seduce some girl. To set an example.

What if there had been any paparazzi around? It may have been night, but you never knew where they may be. What if she was a reporter? Matt remembered the notebook and camera he'd seen her with on the beach, which had instantly raised his suspicions.

And yet there had been something about her... Even hungover, in a blur of pain and self-condemnation, he couldn't help remembering a pair of shining eyes.

The phone was flashing by the bed, he'd missed several messages. He knew who they were from. Miggy. She had also left several messages with the hotel concierge.

She was supposed to be in the middle of filming. He'd wanted a break from it all, to clear his head. Wives and girlfriends weren't joining them on this part of the tour.

He should have been glad, he supposed, that Miggy was calling him. After all there were plenty of men who would have liked to be in his shoes, dating her. She was a celebrity IT-girl and occasional model, and as a high profile couple they were rarely out of the tabloids.

But the more unanswered messages she'd left, the more annoyed with him she would be getting and the less he felt like returning her calls. Matt was also bracing himself to face the team this morning. Hopefully most of them would be even worse for wear and nothing would get said.

What goes on tour stays on tour. For the first time, Matt personally hoped the tenet held true.

Despite his better intentions he found himself casting an eye out for Cara at breakfast. He told himself that it was just to check she was who she said she was - just a tourist - and not busy filing some "Cheating Cricket Love-Rat" exclusive for one of the tabloids.

But he couldn't totally kid himself that was why he was looking. Or that he wasn't disappointed that she didn't appear.

A couple of his team mates joined him at his table and he faced the expected ribbing. Jokes about playing away, and Miggy having his head on the railings. She wasn't known for having an easy temper.

Matt trusted them not to say anything back home but his nerves were on edge.

"You going to see her again?" one of the bowlers asked him.

"I will if you won't," another said. Matt gritted his teeth at the tone.

"No, you bloody won't," he said. The thought of it strangely revulsed him, even though he was used to hearing of good-time girls that worked their way around half the team. "You can concentrate on the game."

He knew he didn't sound convincing, all the more when there were raised eyebrows and further grins. "Miggy's got competition then?"

"There's nothing going on, just drop it. Forget it," he told them and left. He was determined to forget it. He needed to improve his act and start comporting himself like their captain, setting an example to the younger lads instead of behaving like the worst player out there.

* * *

They had kissed for what seemed like hours, though of course it couldn't have been.

Then he'd asked her back to his room, and she'd panicked and fled. Well, not literally fled but she had returned to her own room very quickly.

What must he think of her? Letting him kiss her before she even knew his name? Practically allowing herself to be seduced by him in the sea, in front of everyone.

Cara blushed for her behaviour a hundred times. Thank goodness it had been dark. Perhaps no one had seen much, or at least wouldn't recognise her. She was going to wear her largest sunglasses from now on and dine in her room.

Yet her mind wouldn't stop replaying everything that had happened. How her skin shivered with delight when his hands encircled her waist. How her stomach had jolted when his lips came down on hers. The burning intensity in his eyes.

How much she had wanted him. She had never felt anything like that kind of abandoned, physical longing for Declan. With Matt it had been like a thirst she needed to quench.

She realised she was smiling, just thinking of it all. Perhaps everyone should have a fling once in their lives, to get it out of their system, she thought.

She was a free agent after all. She owed nothing to anyone, least of all Declan. What had happened had happened. She would put it down to too much drink and too much sun. And too much moonlight.

Having skipped breakfast Cara ordered a fruit juice in the hotel lobby. It was a tranquil place at this time of day, with palms and flowers in large pots forming an indoor garden. An elderly couple, whom she'd seen in the dining room the night before, greeted her. They were sitting at a nearby table, the man wearing a Panama hat and reading a newspaper, and the woman doing some knitting.

"Exciting to be staying at the same hotel as the England players, isn't it? We had no idea they'd be here," the woman said to her.

"What England players?" Cara was confused.

"The England cricket team. Surely you've seen them about the place?"

A horrible realisation was starting to dawn on Cara.

Matt… Cricket…

She glanced at the back of the man's newspaper, where the sporting pages were, and saw a photo of the man she'd been kissing last night.

She didn't need to read his full name, though there it was in print. Matt Curran, England captain.

"Are you alright dear? You look a little shaken," the woman said.

"I'm quite fine," Cara tried to reassure her. She wasn't fine at all. The man she had been all over last night, publicly, was the captain of the England cricket team.

Even though she didn't follow cricket she knew who he was, and whom he dated. His girlfriend was even more famous than he was. He was completely off limits. Completely out of her league. It made her feel even trashier about her behaviour the previous night. That day, in fact, since it had been in the early hours of the morning when she had finally parted from him.

"Excuse me," she said to the couple, and rushed back to her room, her eyes blurring with tears of mortification.

Not looking where she was going, Cara collided with someone for the second time that week.

And she knew, almost before she bumped into him, that it was Matt Curran.

* * *

"Are you a reporter?"

He knew as soon as he blurted it out that it was the worst thing to say, let alone in such an aggressive tone.

"No, why?" Cara was completely confused. Why did he look so angry, so suspicious? His bronzed face was rigid, unyielding. He looked even more furious than he had done on the beach.

Yet she couldn't stop looking at his lips. Remembering how they felt on hers, wanting him all over again. She bit her lip and tried to maintain her composure. What did one say in this sort of circumstance?

"Was this some sort of sting? Are you working for one of the tabloids?" he asked, his tone no less demanding then before.

Cara was bewildered. "No, I'm just here on holiday." She didn't know what else to say.

They stood there for a moment, both at a loss. She was looking into his eyes and beyond his distrust she could see a deep weariness.

He saw that he had made her embarrassed and uncomfortable, and it affected him more than he would have liked.

Matt broke the awkward silence.

"Last night..." he faltered, he wasn't even sure what he wanted to say anymore.

"...was a mistake," she finished for him. "I'm sorry, I have to be somewhere." She had nowhere to be, nowhere to go since her room was in the opposite direction and she could hardly turn back past him now. She hurried off, her eyes blurring with tears.

He wanted to call after her but there were people around and making a scene would be even worse. He saw her slight figure moving into the distance.

If she was a reporter he just had totally screwed himself. And if she wasn't a reporter he had just been unconscionably rude to her. Either way, he was going to have to seek her out and apologise to her.

And given the reaction he felt whenever he encountered her, seeking her out would be playing with fire.

3. An apology

They had training that morning but Matt's heart wasn't in it. He was too hungover and stressed with everything that had happened. And even more stressed about what he had to do: apologise to the girl.

After arriving back at the hotel and showering he looked out for her but couldn't see her. He couldn't ask anyone where she was since that would only create greater complications.

He was supposed to be having lunch with the rest of the team but he wanted to clear his head. His preferred method for doing this was to go for a walk, so he set off through the nature park behind the hotel.

Being surrounded by nature in the cooler shade of palms and other tropical plants was soothing and by the time he reached a clearing he was much calmer than he had been all day.

Until, of course, he saw the girl again. Cara. She was sitting on a bench by herself, reading. Didn't she have any friends? Was she here alone?

It was now or never, and he owed her some kind of explanation, so he went over to her and sat down next to her.

"I wanted to apologise for earlier." He didn't have any excuses, not ones that she would understand anyway, so he didn't offer any. "I was rude. I had no reason to be."

He wasn't sure what reaction he was expecting but it wasn't this, a shy and grateful smile, and it made his heart turn over despite himself.

"I didn't realise who you were," she said. "Until breakfast when someone pointed you out."

There was an awkward silence again. They were both aware that he wasn't free to do what he had done, he had known all along and now Cara knew. He had led her on, if anything. She had hardly led him on. What an idiot he had been to even suspect her.

"I'm sorry about the reporter thing," he told her. "That stuff tends to happen, and I was on edge." He knew as he spoke how ridiculous it had been. If she had been aiming at a kiss-and-tell, or some kind of honey-trap, she would hardly have turned him down the previous night.

Why had she turned him down? Matt wasn't used to being turned down, and if he was going to be honest with himself it had partly added to his frustrations.

But looking at her it was obvious why. She was younger than he had first imagined and was clearly not the kind of jaded, groupie type who usually hung around sports teams.

"I promise you I'm nothing do to with newspapers or anything. I'm a student," she said.

She didn't owe him any promise and he felt bad that he had put her in a position where she felt the need to reassure him. She had such honest eyes as well. They showed every emotion, which was why he could tell how much he had hurt and embarrassed her.

But Matt found himself looking from her eyes to her lips. They were full, sensuous and slightly parted. Before he knew what he was doing he was running his hand down the side of her face, cupping her jaw, gently tilting her head up to meet his lips as they came down on hers.

This time this kiss hit him like a shockwave. It was like being back at school again, she reminded him of the first girl he'd ever kissed. The thrill, the excitement, the innocence.

His other arm went around her, drawing her closer to him.

She was such a relief, such an escape. So different to everything else in his life. He felt free of everything with her, even though she was actually complicating things even more than before.

Cara felt like she was drowning as Matt kissed her. Her stomach was flipping over, and she thrilled in the warmth of him and the taste of him.

He's doing this by choice, she thought. He's sober. He's deliberately kissing me. But why, if he had been so angry about it before?

She relaxed into his embrace as they explored one another, drinking one another in. Her arms went around his neck and she once again felt his hair, dry this time, and his sun-warmed skin.

Matt Curran, England cricket captain, was kissing her. It was the strangest and most wonderful thing in the world. She should have felt guilty - after all he had a girlfriend - but right now it felt like they were the only two people in the world. Everyone else, everything, was so far away.

He broke off the kiss but still held her, and was gazing into her eyes.

"This is wrong and very unfair on you," he said. "I'm not a free agent."

"I know."

"You make me wish I was," he told her. Though it wasn't just this girl that made him wish he was single again, he had been growing tired of the complications in his life for some time.

"If all we have is now, is that enough for you?" he asked.

What was he asking her? Was he asking her to have a holiday fling with him?

Two days ago Cara would have been shocked at herself for even considering it, but now she couldn't even bring herself to not consider it.

"It's enough."

"I don't want to lead you on, create expectations," Matt said.

Cara smiled at him. "I wasn't expecting any of this anyway." When she went home it would probably seem like a dream. No one would believe her even if she did tell them. Girls like her didn't date international sports stars, after all. That was the domain of pop stars and glamour models.

"I want to see you tonight. Take you out. But we'll have to be discreet," he said.

The thickness in his voice, the urgency, made her stomach flip all over again.

"Won't you get recognised?" she asked him.

"Perhaps. But if we go somewhere there are only locals, not tourists, it should be safe enough."

Cara had no idea how they were going to leave the hotel together without anyone seeing. "Will your team mates know?"

"If they do, they won't say anything." He was about to say "what goes on tour…" but stopped himself as it sounded sleazy and as though he did this kind of thing all the time. In fact he had been faithful to Miggy since they'd started dating, even though he could never be quite sure of the same loyalty on her side.

Why me? Cara wanted to say. Why was he taking this huge risk to spend an evening with her? If it was something he did all the time, why had he been so paranoid about her being a reporter?

And what would his expectations be? She suddenly felt nervous. Did he just want dinner, and maybe a kiss goodnight? Or would she be expected to offer up more? And what was she comfortable with?

He saw the conflicted emotions across her face. "If you change your mind, it's OK. I don't want to complicate things for you. I just really want to be with you. And even though this sounds like the oldest line in the book, this honestly isn't something I do regularly. At all, in fact."

She had guessed that already but it was reassuring to hear him say it.

"So I'll meet you in the hotel lobby at seven? I have some things to take care of with the team this afternoon, so I need to get back."

Before he went he kissed her again and she could feel the heat between them.

As he walked back she watched him, noting how athletic he was with his broad shoulders and muscular legs. Once again she marvelled that she had met him in this way. It felt quite surreal.

* * *

For the rest of the afternoon Cara tried to block out her whirling thoughts with study. Principles of Biochemistry was a mental cold shower at the best of times, and forcing herself to focus on its contents was as effective as anything at forcing the image of Matt from her mind.

She was trying to think only about details, about the short term. She didn't want to think about the afterwards, and how irresponsible she was doubtless being for agreeing to go out with him that night.

What should she wear? Which shoes? Should she pin her hair up or let it loose? Unimportant, feminine concerns to distract herself from the bigger picture.

Eventually she chose a pale blue sundress that showed off her tan. She loosely pinned up her hair, letting a few tendrils fall down. Her skin was already sun-kissed so she wore minimal make up.

She wished she had a girlfriend there to give her an assessment and some moral support. But her best friend Ann was back in the UK and almost certainly wouldn't approve of something like this, engaged to a trainee vicar as she was.

The fact that she was completely alone gave Cara a strange sense of freedom. Nothing on this holiday would count, she decided. It was out of time, out of her world, the equivalent to a dream. She would follow her desires and when she went home again she would be back to normality and it would be nothing but a memory, a secret that no one need ever know about.

It was an adventure. Below the calm and collected manner she was trying to project, her stomach was churning with nerves, both fear and excitement.

And something deeper. Some strange, fatalistic sense that something was happening in her life that was actually supposed to happen. That although this all should seem wrong, it felt right. This encounter was meant to be.

4. An enchanted evening

From the moment she met him in the lobby, Cara knew she had made the right decision.

It wasn't just that he was wearing a shirt the exact same colour of her dress, a coincidence that made them both laugh and broke the tension.

It was that when she saw him he was Matt, someone who should really be a total stranger but felt like the exact right person to be with. Her co-conspirator. Her partner-in-crime.

Someone whose smile made her weak at the knees and whose touch, as he lightly held her arm as they went to a taxi, made her skin tingle.

"I was worried you'd stand me up," he told her later. She was surprised to see there was genuine uncertainty in his eyes. He couldn't be used to girls standing him up, surely?

"It was a hard choice between you and the hotel seafood buffet," Cara said.

"The seafood buffet is every night," Matt said and she laughed again.

The taxi driver took them some miles out of the city, away from the coast and into the hills, until they came to a tiny restaurant in such a secluded spot that Cara wondered how it managed to get any clientele.

Her stomach was turning over with nerves and she wasn't sure why. Was it the fear of being seen with him? Was it being with him? Was it a sense of the forbidden?

Cara let Matt order the food as he seemed to be more acquainted with the local cuisine than she was. As a cricketer he had travelled the world and was doubtless used to exotic places, she supposed. Her travels didn't extend much beyond summer holidays to France and Spain. This was the furthest she had ever been from home.

In more ways than one. She was out of her element here, voyaging into the unknown.

Matt started asking Cara about her life. His head told him that this was a mistake, it would be better to keep things superficial and remain strangers as far as possible. But he wanted to know more about her. She intrigued him - his reaction to her intrigued him - and he was trying to figure out why.

There wasn't much to tell, Cara felt. School, then university. It wasn't as though she had even started a proper career yet.

She didn't want to tell him about Declan, but he managed to coax it out of her. She gave him the very bare basics: that there had been someone, but she had recently broken it off.

"Was it serious?" he asked.

"I thought it was at one time, but not now."

"How serious? Living together?"

"No, but we were engaged," Cara told him.

"Surely you're a bit young for that?"

That was what her friends had said. "Maybe. Not that it matters now."

Matt saw a shadow pass over her face and felt bad for asking her. The thought of Cara being engaged made him uneasy, partly because he was still trying to keep Miggy at arm's length and delay what everyone assumed was inevitable.

Added to that, Cara was also considerably younger than Miggy from what he could work out. He hadn't asked her what her age was, but from what she had said about her life so far she couldn't be much past her early twenties.

There was something else that made him uneasy about the topic of her being engaged, but he didn't want to think about that. So he changed the subject to ask her about more neutral things. What she thought of Sri Lanka, where she had travelled.

Because there wasn't much to say, Cara eventually turned the questioning onto him. "So how did you get into playing cricket?" It was probably something any cricket fan would know, but he already knew she wasn't a cricket fan due to her failure to recognise him or any of the team on their first encounters.

He gave her a potted history, the same he gave in any interview. Schoolboy cricket, university cricket, county selection.

"What's it like, playing cricket?" Cara asked him. "I mean internationally, as a career?"

No one had ever asked Matt this. For a moment he was lost in thought just at this fact. He'd been asked any amount of times about how he was feeling ahead of a match or after a match, what he thought about an umpiring decision or his own performance, for his thoughts on other teams and players, endless thorny questions about cricket politics and the future of the game. He'd been asked personal questions: about his relationships, his family, his plans for the future. But never this.

Had he even thought about it himself? What was it like, playing cricket, being an international sportsman? An easy answer was to say it was a dream come true but that didn't really explain what it was like.

"It's strange, I guess. You're always on the road, travelling, spending all your time with the team. But everyone else has their own family lives as well. It's a very short career of course. You spend your first years worrying about selection and your later years worrying about injury and retirement."

"But you love it?"

He did. More than anything. More than being with Miggy, if truth be told. There never seemed to be time to step back and reflect, but doing so now Matt realised how grateful he was. He found himself thinking about a boyhood friend who had played alongside him in the under-19 team and for a couple of seasons of country cricket. He hadn't made it to the big time and had ended up selling real estate. "Yes. I feel very lucky."

"And actually playing matches, what's that like?" Cara asked. She was genuinely interested.

Once again Matt had to think about it. It was just something he did, not something he considered. "You're very focused, it's tactical. We spend so much time training and preparing. Probably just like anything except there's more at stake with a test match."

"It must be hard when it's going badly."

It was. Having to go out on a pitch day after day, half way through a series you were already losing, knowing the odds were against you. Knowing the savaging the press back home would deliver. No wonder he was so wary of journalists.

"It's not the greatest. I think this tour will go alright though."

Then he was silent for a moment, looking into her eyes. This tour already felt different than others had, though he didn't want to admit why.

Cara looked back at him. They held the gaze longer than they should have. The air felt charged with electricity. Deeper than that, she felt a connection with him.

Matt also felt as though for the first time in a long time, someone was actually looking at him. Matt Curran the person. Not the sports star, the captain, the famous international player. Just a man. He felt oddly exposed and wasn't sure if he was comfortable with it.

She was so pretty though. He liked the way she seemed both shy and spirited.

The waiter appeared to top up their drinks, breaking the tension. Cara hadn't planned to drink much at all, intending to have her wits fully about her. But she could already feel a warm glow and an increased sense of recklessness. The little stern voice inside her head, telling her to be sensible, to not get in over her head, was being drowned out.

It wasn't just the alcohol making her giddy though. It was the proximity to this man, with his masculine good looks, his tall, athletic body, and the strangely haunted look that she sometimes saw in his eyes. A look of doubt. But she wasn't sure what he doubted. Did he still not trust that she really was who she said she was?

Matt was wrestling with himself. He knew what he wanted to do that night. He also knew what he should do. It was funny, thinking back how just a few years ago he would have had no qualms. Everything would have been so easy. Was this exciting because it was illicit? Complicated? Did he want to pursue this girl because it was forbidden?

All he could be certain of was that for the first time in ages, he was seriously tempted. More that tempted in fact because he was going to pursue this. He was already doing so, he had already taken a huge risk just coming here with her.

The vision of a boy, over a decade ago, sprang into his mind. Arriving home and embracing his mother. "I met a girl!" His mother laughing, pleased. Her face lighting up with gladness for him.

He could hardly remember that girl's name now. They had barely been out of their teens, it hadn't lasted.

It hadn't started that way with Miggy. Their relationship had burst into the tabloids almost from the outset, before he'd even had time to think. He remembered feeling almost furtive when he told his parents he was "seeing someone" and they told him that they already knew. Everyone knew.

He didn't remember his mother's face lighting up. Maybe her expression was neutral. Maybe she had been worried, even. For a wild moment he wanted his time back. To be free. To be able to tell them he'd met someone, with all the joy and hope of that first time.

"Are you alright?" Cara was looking at him, concerned.

"Just lost in the past for a moment."

"You look tired. Did you want to get back? I know you must have an early start tomorrow."

He wanted to get back but not for the early start. He wanted to get back to the hotel and lose himself in this girl. He wanted to drown out his problems and his memories and right now he felt that she was the perfect drug to do that.

Whether she was up for it was another matter. But he was going to try his chances.

5. Breaking boundaries

They got a taxi back to the hotel. Matt sat in the back with Cara, and neither of them spoke. Cara was boiling with nerves in case he made a move. She knew she would have to decline but she wasn't sure how that might go.

She started as she felt his hand move over hers. He made no other move, he just held her hand until they were back at the Pavilion hotel. After he paid the driver he walked with her back into the lobby.

"I'm not going to ask you to come up for a nightcap because it would be blatantly obvious I didn't just want a drink," he said. "But I would like you to come up. I don't want this evening to end just yet and it's not private here."

Cara didn't want the evening to end either. For a moment she wavered, feeling as though she was on one side of a line that probably shouldn't be crossed.

"I can come up for a bit," she said.

They went up in the elevator to his floor, which was higher up than hers. He opened the door and ushered her in.

Like her room it was immaculate. The sheets taut and pristine over the bed. Anything that Matt might have left strewn around was tidied away by the chambermaids.

He had a sea view from his balcony, the same as hers, and she went over to the window to look at the ocean. The moon shone silver on the waters.

She felt him step behind her. His arms went around her and for a moment they stood there.

Then he turned her towards him, wordlessly, and brushed a curl of hair off her face.

The next moment his lips were on hers, hard, urgent. She felt her body swoon into his kiss almost like a kind of relief. His tongue was probing her, exploring her and she reciprocated.

Cara was glad that the room was dark. He hadn't turned any lights on, the only illumination came from lights outside and the moon over the ocean.

Her head was swimming. She was alone with this man in his room, it was clear where things were leading.

And she wanted him badly.

His hand supported the small of her back as he continued to embrace her. He kissed down her neck and onto her shoulder, slipping down the thin strap so her skin was bare against his lips.

She ran her hands over his back, feeling the heat of his skin through his shirt and the muscle of his back. He was so much taller and stronger than her. Knowing his superior strength - how she was literally in his hands - gave her a shivery feeling in the pit of her stomach.

She could smell the heat of him, the faint trace of soap, the maleness.

Matt ran his fingers through her hair, freeing it so it tumbled down loose about her shoulders. Cara felt wanton: her dress nearly slipping off, her hair unbound.

Then his hand moved to her ribs, his thumb brushing the side of her breast as he held her to him. His hands were strong yet gentle, insistent but not hurting her.

Somehow he manoeuvred her towards the bed, pushing her down onto the white covers. He was firm but not rough.

Her hair was spilling over the pillow and she looked up into his eyes, dark in the dim light, but she could still see the intensity there. Because she felt the same.

Slowly he slipped her dress down, exposing her bra, down to her stomach. He unclasped it and ran his hands over her breasts, her naked skin thrilling to his touch.

"God you're beautiful," he told her.

Before she could find words to respond to him his lips were on hers again, passionate, tasting her, teasing her. He trailed kisses down her throat, over the top of her breasts. His mouth went over her nipple and drew it in and she cried out.

His other hand was on her wrist, holding her arm above her head, pinning her down while he devoured her body. Cara was helpless with desire for him.

Then both his hands were on her dress, pulling it all the way down. Just a thin triangle of silk covered her from him.

Matt was still fully clothed, and for a moment he pressed himself against her. She felt the cotton of his shirt crushed against her body, the fabric of his jeans along her legs. His long, hard thigh muscles. His athletic weight.

He covered her. He was kissing her, enjoying the feeling of having this naked girl below him, willing and desiring of him as he was of her.

But he wanted to feel her body directly against his. He ripped off his shirt and moulded her against him. Their mutual heat burned.

Cara adored the feeling of him on top of her. She couldn't move - he was weighing her down - but she squirmed and as she did so she felt the hardness of him through his jeans.

It gave her a mental jolt. It was clear what he wanted. Was she ready for this? She tried not to feel nervous but she had no idea how this would go.

Given how long she had delayed this, with Declan wanting to do the old-fashioned thing and have a virgin in his marriage bed, she was unsure if she should let Matt do this to her now. Was it too quick, too soon?

But maybe it was becoming a burden. Maybe it was time she finally let herself go and passed from girlhood to womanhood. Then at least she could decide whether it was worth it.

While she had been thinking these thoughts Matt had stripped off the rest of his clothes. She felt his maleness against her thigh. She sensed how large it was and it made her a little fearful.

Should she tell him this was her first time? She couldn't think of a way to do so that wouldn't be completely awkward. And what if he found it unappealing, or rejected her?

No, it was time for resolve. Her body melted at his touch, her skin was on fire from his caresses and she wanted more of him. She wanted all of him.

Suddenly he had moved down, and his hands moved her thighs apart. Cara had never been this exposed to a man before. She wished she had had a few more drinks to take the edge off her nerves now. But his touch was so electric that she got over her qualms.

She felt him kiss up her inner thigh, toward her centre. Then his lips were on the thin fabric of her underwear, brushing over her sensitive flesh beneath. She could feel the silk clinging to her, growing wet from her own desire and from the heat of his breath.

Then he moved it to the side and worked his way between her lips, his tongue slipping between them. Cara was starting to whimper with pleasure, even though she was still hesitant.

He paused for a moment: "You taste amazing." Then his tongue slid back, flat and firm against her, and he wrapped his arms around her hips to pull her into his mouth.

His hands moved over her breasts as he teased her, going slightly and slowly over her most sensitive nub, slowly building the intensity. He was holding her on the brink and she was pressing against him, wanting and needing more.

He stopped and she nearly wept with wanting him to continue. But his fingers were now hooking through her underwear, drawing it down her thighs, over her legs, pulling off her last defence and barrier.

Matt was already naked and she felt him move her thighs apart with his knees. He was gentle but he was also insistent. He couldn't wait much longer. He was the one in control, and he needed release.

He kissed up her body again, over her breasts, taking her nipple into his mouth and swirling his tongue around it. Sucking it in hard, almost painful, but she still wanted more.

Then she felt his hardness pressing against her. She was so wet and slick from his caresses that despite his size he managed to push inside her easily, just a few millimetres, teasing her by holding back from going further.

Cara was more nervous yet also more weak with desire than she thought possible. This was it. There was no going back. She could see from the dark heat in his gaze how much he needed her. How much he wanted her.

His mouth came down on hers again and he thrust inside her: one long, hard, hot stroke. Despite a momentary pain she felt her body drawing him in and they lay there together for a second, he was fully inside her, as deep and close as he could be. Tight, stretching her around him.

Then he withdrew, slowly, not quite leaving her and pushed back into her, slower again. It still hurt but Cara loved the sensation of him filling her and being deep inside her.

He repeated the long, slow strokes several times and gradually it started to feel easier. The initial discomfort shifted into a warm, sensual ache. She found herself instinctively moving her hips up towards him to feel him even harder and deeper.

It was a union. It was as though they were both trying to be as close to one another as possible, fully joined.

Matt's body was so closely pressed against hers that when he rocked into her, he was grinding against her most sensitive area. Each time Cara felt herself gasp as the pressure built there, wanting and needing more and more.

Now he was increasing his speed and the hardness of his thrusts. His head was buried in her neck, she felt him murmur something but she couldn't make it out.

He raised himself above her, still driving into her, making her nearly sob from the sensation.

"Christ Cara..." He could barely speak. "You are so incredible..."

Cara looked up at his face, his skin and hair damp from the heat generated between them as hers was. She was awed that she had such an effect on him.

She had been worried that she wouldn't be able to satisfy him due to her lack of experience. But his obvious reaction to her - the intensity with which he was pushing into her - clearly showed his desire.

It erased her anxieties. It allowed her to let herself go, to abandon herself to the sensations he was arousing in her body.

His hands were on her breasts, his lips once again on hers.

Faster, harder.

Then just as she thought her body couldn't be wound up any more she felt like she was falling. A bright, white light flickered out from between her legs and uncoiled throughout her stomach, radiating to the sensitive buds of her nipples that he was fondling. Everything was tight, drawn, connected.

She could hear herself crying out but it was like hearing someone else. Matt drew in his breath sharply and suddenly arched his back, gripped her hips and thrust into her as deep as he could go. He held himself there, not letting her go, forcing her against his body.

She felt him swell, become harder than ever, then pulse within her.

Then he collapsed on her, both of them wet, sated, exhausted. They lay there for a while recovering.

Then Matt rolled over to one side. His arm was still across Cara's body and he left it there. "Stay with me."

She looked at him but before she could respond she saw that his eyes were already closed. He was sleeping.

Not wanting to wake him, she lay there with the weight of his arm keeping her close to him. Her head was still whirling, her body tingling and rushing. But the sound of his even breathing began to soothe her, and soon she fell asleep beside him.

6. Playing the game

Cara awoke in the early hours, around dawn. She could see the sky growing lighter over the sea. Matt was fast asleep, in a deep, heavy slumber, and barely stirred when she carefully lifted his arm off her.

She wasn't sure quite what she should do, but she suspected it would be very awkward if he woke up and she was there. After all it was only supposed to be a casual thing. And he had to play a cricket match in a few hours' time.

Lying there, only half covered by the sheets, he looked like a sculpted bronze statue. Cara allowed herself one more gaze, trying to capture it in her mind so she would remember him always, slipped on her clothes and crept out.

Back in her room she showered, and then tried to go to sleep again for a couple of hours. But it was impossible: her mind was whirling.

She wanted to avoid him and the rest of the players at all costs, so she hid away in her room and tried to do some study until she was sure they must have breakfasted and been long gone to the cricket match. Then and only then did she finally put on a new outfit for the day and venture downstairs.

As she passed the lobby to the veranda, where she planned to order a strong coffee, the concierge hailed her. "Madam, there is some post for you."

Cara's first thought was that he meant post from overseas, and had a moment of consternation. Was there an emergency back home? But no, surely they would have telephoned if there had been. For one moment she wondered if it was from Declan, until the concierge handed her a plain white envelope with no address and no stamp.

She took it to the veranda with her and opened it.

It contained two tickets to the test match that day.

Only Matt could have sent it. It must mean he wanted her to come. His team mates wouldn't have put them there for a prank, would they? Surely none of them knew, she was confident no one had seen them leave the hotel together the previous evening nor return together.

As she sat there, her emotions conflicted as to what to do, the elderly English couple passed her table. "We're just off to watch the cricket," the man told her. He noticed the tickets that Cara was holding. "Are you coming along too? Why don't you share a ride with us?"

That settled it. Cara could hardly say she wasn't going without generating curiosity. She thanked them, and got up to go.

"Do you need to wait for a companion?" the woman asked. Cara was confused, then realised she was holding two tickets.

"No, it's just me. My friend couldn't come," she told them. It was thoughtful of Matt to have sent her two tickets, he must have thought she would have preferred not to go alone. Or maybe he was concerned that if she did go alone, it would arouse suspicion?

At any rate she now had two escorts and it would probably appear to any observers that she was holidaying with the British couple.

In the taxi to the cricket ground they exchanged names. The Hilliers were retired and lived in Surrey. They were both passionate cricket supporters and frequently timed their holidays abroad to coincide with England tours. Cara thought how nice it must be for them to have a shared interest that they had both enjoyed like this.

It reminded her of how little she had had in common with Declan. He liked golf of all things, which bored her to tears. Even if she had shown an interest it was Declan's view that golf wasn't really a game for women to play. At one time she had cherished what she thought of as his old fashioned values.

Now, given his values where his secretary was concerned, she saw everything in a very different light.

"Do you get to watch many of the county cricket games back home?" Mrs Hillier was asking her.

Cara didn't like to admit that she had never been to a match in her life. "Unfortunately not, due to work commitments," she said.

"This will be a nice treat for you then!"

Would it? She wasn't sure if watching cricket would be entertaining or bewildering. From the glimpses she had seen on TV there seemed to be a lot of standing around. But she was determined to go with an open mind. She reflected on how athletic Matt was, as well as the other players she had seen back at the hotel. The game must be reasonably fast-paced and strenuous.

As it turned out she was rapt from the moment they arrived. Matt was batting - she got a jolt seeing his name in large white letters on the scoreboard - and she was on the edge of her seat. It took her a while to get a grasp of the flow of the game, but she remembered a bit from her childhood and her boarding school cousins playing cricket on the lawn. Innings and overs and things. Mrs Hillier generously shared her field glasses with her.

Cara was transfixed by the intensity of the game. It was like chess: the batsmen would hold out, patient, defensive, with the spectators around them getting more and more tense.

Then suddenly there would be an aggressive and spectacular flurry of riskier batting, with the two men putting on another dozen runs and the crowd on their feet whenever the ball was hit for six, before things would settle down again to the endless waiting game.

It was an ordeal. It was fascinating. It was gripping. Cara was absolutely hooked.

As she watched Matt's lean figure from afar, clad in white, his jaw set resolute against the onslaught, she thrilled every time he cracked the ball back with force and precision, fighting his way to fifty runs by the lunchtime break and getting a standing ovation.

"Splendid effort by Curran this morning," Mr Hillier said. "It's going to be an exciting afternoon if he goes for the full century."

As they took their seats again just before the afternoon session started, Cara thought how idyllic the ground was. It overlooked the shining waters of the Indian ocean on east and west, with a historic fort to the south. But the serenity belied the fierce battle waged on its green expanse.

Cara almost wished she hadn't come as the play progressed for the rest of the day. The scoreboard kept climbing and Matt continued to cling on. As his total edged its way upwards the tension in the ground was escalating.

The bowlers were desperate to get him out, you could feel their hunger to defeat him. It was no longer team versus team, it was eleven men versus just one man.

Every appeal - when the Sri Lankan team tried to claim he was out - made her nearly nauseous, and she physically sank back into her chair with relief each time the umpires gave their decision in Matt's favour.

Finally he had reached the nineties, playing cautiously but still bravely, the runs accumulating at an agonisingly slow rate.

Then he was at ninety-six. The bowler hurtled towards him.

Cara nearly closed her eyes but forced herself to watch, to see Matt crack the ball straight over the boundary in his most spectacular shot of the day.

The board flicked over to 102 and the entire stadium was on its feet in uproar. Even the Hilliers were standing up, applauding and cheering in a very British fashion. Cara just felt dazed. She felt emotionally and physically exhausted.

Was it usually like this? How did they all bear it? Completely on edge for six solid hours.

And all this taking place after a night of extremely disrupted sleep, which she now blushed to think about.

* * *

The Hilliers invited Cara to dine with them that night, but she declined and promised to the following evening instead. She was simply too overwhelmed by the day's events, the force of her own reaction to them, and a desire to avoid Matt.

He would be surrounded by people anyway, fêting him for his century.

Cara ordered room service and ate it on her balcony, the tropical sea breezes calming the heat in her body if not her mind.

She had planned to read but was too tired to even do that, so slipped into the freshly made bed and let sleep overtake her.

Drifting into dreams, she was suddenly awoken by a loud rapping at the door.

Confused, and seeing on the illuminated beside alarm clock that it was shortly after eleven o'clock, she pulled a wrap around her and went to answer it.

It was Matt.

"I had to see you," he said. "I looked for you at dinner but you weren't there. Can I come in?"

She ushered him through. "Aren't you exhausted after today?"

"More wired than anything." He didn't look exhausted. He looked resolute.

She thanked him for the tickets. "I hadn't been to a test match before. It was very kind of you."

"Did you enjoy it?" he asked.

What could she say? Had she enjoyed it? It had felt like the biggest ordeal of her life, worse than sitting through the most gruelling exam ever. And yet it had also been the most thrilling and glorious sensation she could remember - the previous night excepted - when he had finally scored one hundred runs.

"It was… amazing."

He laughed. "That's thanks to you. You brought me luck."

She knew he was joking but he continued. "Seriously. Knowing you were there just gave me extra motivation. It gave me an edge that my game has been lacking recently."

"I didn't think you would have known I was there," Cara said.

"I saw you arrive with that couple from the hotel." He put his hands on her shoulders and looked down at her, his gaze intense. "And I need to stay with you tonight."

Her stomach flipped in anticipation. "Wouldn't you prefer a good night's sleep?"

"That's exactly what I'm planning to get." There was a glint in his eye as his lips came down on hers, and Cara felt as though she was melting against him. She marvelled at his stamina after all those hours on the pitch.

He scooped her up and carried her to the bed. "We could use my room, but seeing as this is just as convenient…"

They kissed for a while and then he stopped. "I meant to ask you about something this morning but you ran out on me. You said you'd been engaged, so I just assumed, I mean anyone would assume…"

She knew what he was trying to say and was mortified. Had her inexperience been that noticeable? Had she been that inept in bed?

"Was it very obvious?" she asked.

"No, that's the thing, not until…" He didn't specify and she wanted to die of embarrassment. "It's just that if I'd known, I wouldn't have…"

"…you wouldn't have done it?"

He looked embarrassed. "Probably not. It's not very fair on you, given the circumstances."

"It's too late now, and I don't have any regrets, if that's what you're worried about. It doesn't have to change anything."

He looked relieved though still somewhat guilty. "Also we didn't…"

"It's OK, I'm safe where that's concerned." Cara said hurriedly. She had gone on the pill some months before, in anticipation of Declan possibly breaking his resolve to hold off until their wedding night. Which he had done, just not with her.

"Well then, given that we're both safe…" His lips came down on her again, this time trailing down her neck, the hollows at its base, over her breast and closing over her nipple as he moved the neck of her nightgown down.

She ached for him.

His hand reached lower. Given the heat of the night she wasn't wearing any underwear, and his fingers slipped straight between.

"Do you want me?" he asked her, knowing the answer full well from how wet and ready she was.

"Yes." It was barely a whisper. She needed him.

"On one condition then." He was teasing her as he wanted her just as badly. He could barely hold back. "I want you there every day, at the ground, for this match. I'd fly you to the whole series if I could but you probably have to get back."

Cara was thrilled that he wanted her there but pretended to be non-committal.

"I'll have to see, there might not be any tickets left. Maybe you should remind me what the attraction is…"

He grinned and then turned his full, masterful attention back to her body. It was a long time before either of them got any sleep.

7. On the balcony

Cara awoke. It was still dark and the alarm clock told her it was only just past midnight. Matt was no longer in bed beside her. There was only an empty space with rumpled sheets and she felt a pang.

It was only their third night together but she was already getting used to him, which was dangerous.

Looking up she noticed that the balcony door was open, the curtain billowing gently from the sea breeze. She got up and saw that Matt was standing out there, looking at the ocean. She felt joy and relief surge inside her which was an even more dangerous sign.

He turned his head and saw her. "I didn't wake you, did I?"

"No. Have you been awake long?"

"Just a few minutes. Come and join me."

Winding a sheet around her Cara stepped outside and stood against the railing next to him. He put his arm around her, his hand resting gently in the curve of her lower back. She was surprised and happy at the intimacy.

"One of the perks of the job. This…" he indicated the sea, sky and stars. It was one of those tropical nights that people describe as velvet: an ink-black sky with night air warm enough that even the sea breezes didn't chill the skin. A pale gold moon, shining on the waters.

"It must be interesting, all the travel," Cara said.

"It is. I wanted a job where you could see the world. I studied engineering at university, I had ideas of working in the Middle East if cricket didn't happen."

"Have you been there?"

"Only as a tourist, a week in Dubai," Matt said. "What about you, with biochemistry?" He had seen the textbooks on the table in her room.

"The same, actually." One of the reasons Cara had chosen it was for the research opportunities overseas. Years ago she had visited Geneva on a school trip and dreamt of living there one day. She told Matt this.

"How's your Swiss?"

"French, in that part," Cara told him. "I'd have to brush up. Do you pick up different languages on tour?"

"Mainly expletives at the stumps. If I ever need to swear fluently in Urdu I'm set."

Cara laughed.

Matt looked at her, her eyes shining, her hair loose. She was so beautiful and natural. So easy to be with. If it was a different time in his life, if they were both in different places... but there was no point thinking about it. It was something to enjoy for the moment.

"Would you like a drink?" he asked. "I'm a million miles from sleep but I have to be up in a few hours. I could do with something to knock me out."

"I can see what's in the minibar," Cara said.

"Let's go up to my room, then we can raid it properly. My tab gets covered."

Cara slipped on a robe and Matt pulled his clothes on and they crept along the corridor to the lift. If anyone was up at this hour of the night and encountered them it would be disastrous. It felt like they were co-conspirators, the risk adding an extra frisson.

When they got to Matt's room, immaculately made up by the chambermaid earlier that day and still untouched, he put his arms around her and kissed her. "The drink can wait."

They tumbled onto the bed, finally giving the pillows and sheets a proper creasing. Cara adored the proximity of him, being in his arms, being touched by him, just being with him.

Afterwards he was lying on top of her for a few moments and she thought he was falling asleep but then he rolled off her.

If anything should have helped knock him out it was making love to her yet again, but instead he felt reenergised. He rifled through the minibar and picked out a tiny bottle. "Brandy always makes me sleepy." He offered one to Cara but she chose a mineral water.

They went outside onto Matt's balcony and sat in the two chairs on either side of the balcony table. Cara felt that her body was tired, after the long day in the sun of watching the game, the excitement, the vigorous attentions of Matt a couple of hours earlier. But her mind was completely awake and alert. She knew if she went straight back to bed she would simply lie there, sleepless.

"How long do you think you'll play cricket for?" Cara asked him. "When do most players retire?"

"It varies, it tends to be a bit earlier for bowlers. I should have another good five years. Assuming no injury, of course," Matt said.

"What will you do afterwards?"

Coaching or commentating were the obvious routes, but Matt really hadn't decided. As a former captain he would have more doors open to him than the average international player. It depended how much he wanted to keep travelling as well. "Probably something related to cricket still. I can't see myself opening a bar or going back into engineering..."

As he spoke the door buzzed and there was a loud knocking. Cara froze in shock.

"Ignore it," Matt said. "Someone drunk, probably."

But the loud raps continued. "Just wait here," he told her. Cara moved to the end of the balcony so the curtain screened her from the door.

Matt's first thought was that it was some drunken cricket fan, there were a few around that tended to drink beer every night and get rowdy. He opened the door and Jeremy and two other cricketers piled in before he could stop them.

They were all off their faces drunk, waving bottles of booze. Too drunk at least to notice what he had been up to, he hoped.

They sprawled all over the bed and chairs.

"What the hell are you playing at? We've got play in a few hours," Matt said.

"Don't be so uptight, we'll hammer them." This was met with cheers and bottles clinked together in toast.

What the hell was he going to do? It would be more than awkward if he was discovered. He should be able to trust them but he couldn't guarantee there wouldn't be gossip. Gossip that was bound to trickle back to the UK papers.

"Have a drink!" A half drunk bottle of wine was pushed at Matt but he put it down on a side table out of reach.

"Get out, all of you, and try and sober up by morning. For Christ's sake…"

"Why are you so keen to get rid of us? Got company?" One of them got up and pretended to look in the bathroom, and then started taking a leak.

Outside Cara could hear what was going on and was terrified for both their sakes. She couldn't see what was happening but she recognised Jeremy's voice and those of the others. What if they decided to lumber out onto the balcony?

She shrank into the furthest corner, and looked around for some kind of escape. She could climb onto the next balcony - the doors there were closed so presumably the occupants were asleep - and at least duck down and hide there until Matt gave the all clear.

Cara wasn't a huge fan of heights but she plucked up her courage.

Clambering onto the rail and over the neighbouring rail in a skimpy night robe, trying not to look down at the narrow but precipitous gap between them, was no easy feat.

By the time she had crouched down below sight level on the other balcony she was trembling with relief and the stress of the ordeal. The curtains were drawn behind the sliding glass doors which was good. She just kept as quiet as she could, and listened.

Sure enough one of the players noticed the open door and wandered out onto the balcony while Matt was trying to get them all out of his room. He wasn't too drunk to overlook the two glasses.

"Been entertaining?" he asked Matt.

"They're both mine. One to dilute the other, which it's a pity you lot haven't been doing." Matt tried to sound convincing.

Where the hell was Cara? Surely she couldn't have jumped? He looked across at the rooms either side. It would be possible to climb over but you'd have to have some nerve. Was she hiding on one of them? He desperately hoped so.

Fear giving him greater resolve, he finally managed to strong arm the player off the balcony, drag the others off the bed and manoeuvre them in the direction of the door. "Now get the hell out and don't wake up the rest of the hotel."

Matt knew there were journalists in the hotel, quite apart from cricket officials who would not look favourably on England players being drunk and disorderly mid-test.

He was also annoyed because they had been strongly set to win the first test - not least due to his own century in the first innings - and something like this could derail the game totally.

But there were more pressing matters. Where was Cara? Ensuring his door was locked he went back outside and called her, in a whisper.

"I'm here." She stood up, revealing herself on the next balcony. He felt physical relief as his estimation of her soared: it must have taken guts.

"Can you make it back over? Let me give you a hand."

The return climb was infinitely worse because it had all hit her and she was shaky with it, and she was no longer fortified by the initial adrenalin. It took an enormous summoning of nerve to force herself to get back across but she tried not to let him know. She froze momentarily as she was over the gap and had to force herself to keep going.

She practically tumbled onto Matt's balcony and he helped her up and she fell against him, barely able to stand. She clung to him and he wrapped his arms around her tightly.

Finally they were both laughing about it. He was impressed by how quickly she recovered. She had courage, this girl.

"Do you want a drink now? I know you didn't before, but I need a strong one more than ever after that."

She let him pour her some brandy and then finally exhausted they fell into bed together and slept until morning. "Stay with me,

I'll have more peace of mind if you're still here when I leave," he asked her.

This wasn't quite true. What was true was that he wanted to wake up with her. He didn't want to wake up with an empty bed and a space where she had been, like that first morning.

Like it or not, the experience had also brought them closer together. If they had felt like co-conspirators before, they were a team now. Temporary, of course, but the ordeal had created a bond that Matt hadn't anticipated.

8. After hours action

There were three highly sober and contrite players at breakfast the next morning. To say they looked the worse for wear would be an understatement. Figuring that having to play for hours in the sun with a hangover would be punishment enough, and buoyed with relief over not being discovered, Matt let it go. "Just hold off until the end of the week next time," he told them.

Regardless of the drama last night, Matt was feeling content. Happy, even, though his focus on the test series tended to keep his mood serious. His game was better than it had been in ages. The team was in form. The press were supportive. There were no heavy politics distracting him behind the scenes.

And he hadn't heard from Miggy in days which was a welcome break for his peace of mind.

Not only that, he was enjoying the most amazing nights with an incredibly sweet and beautiful girl. He knew it couldn't last, and he knew it wasn't serious, but occasionally he smiled just thinking about her. She might not have Miggy's worldly sophistication but she was fun to be with and at times when he had been momentarily stressed, she had made him laugh. Lifted his mood.

Miggy used to be able to make him laugh. She would endlessly regale him with anecdotes of various famous people who moved in the same circles she did. At first he had found it fascinating, amusing. But after a while it started to pall. So what if another eighties popstar had got into a fight with a TV actor at a party? Or a peer of the realm had been caught with his trousers down in a lap dancing club? After a while it simply wasn't interesting any more.

Cara didn't know anyone and instead of finding this dull Matt found it refreshing. Being with her was an escape, a relief. It was real. She may not have had Miggy's experience, but she was generous and willing in bed. He found himself lost in her in a way that shut out the rest of the world and any stress or worry he had.

With Miggy it was all about her. They talked about her thoughts, her friends, her problems, never his. She understood Matt couldn't drop what he was doing cricket-wise to be with her, she wasn't that self-centred, but everything else they did was her choice, her preference. She'd also drop their plans like a stone if a last minute job came up, such as her trip to Peru during the previous test series. Which Matt figured was fair enough as she had her own career to think of, but he sometimes felt taken for granted.

Whereas Cara had been interested in him. Genuinely wanting to know about him, and what he thought about things. She was smart. She could talk about science, which Matt appreciated as his own degree had been in engineering.

He shouldn't be comparing them, he supposed, it wasn't fair on either of them. It wasn't as though it was either or. It was Cara now, a brief and enjoyable overseas fling, and then back to Miggy and regular life when the tour finally ended.

But standing there, on the pitch, thinking about what he wanted to do afterwards to unwind, it was only ever Cara that came into his mind.

* * *

Cara was still pinching herself daily, feeling as though she was in some wonderful and forbidden dream. She knew that she absolutely must not fall for Matt but trying to discipline her thoughts and feelings to stay platonic was not easy. They were taking a huge risk regardless, as the intrusion in Matt's room the other night had demonstrated.

Matt wasn't available. He had been clear about that. He was in a high profile relationship with a famous model, and when Cara went back home she would have to put all this behind her and move on. Wrap her memories up in a box and store them away, like putting old photos in the attic.

"Every girl should have a secret affair," an elderly aunt of hers had once said.

Aunt Diana probably hadn't intended a full blown affair in the sense it was understood today though. She had meant something far more chaste and reserved, carried out through love letters and dances at chaperoned balls, tragically ended by some misfortune or forced separation. Leaving nothing behind but a few billets-doux and dried rose petals to grow misty-eyed over in old age.

What would Cara's mementoes be? A few faded photos - none directly of Matt, of course - and the ticket stubs to a long-ago test match.

But right now it wasn't time to think about that. It was time to simply enjoy the moment.

They couldn't be seen together by other people, since although Matt trusted his team mates, the more people who knew about it just made it riskier. Plus there were journalists around the place. If he had been single, or even just one of the team, it might not have mattered. But as captain he was under more scrutiny.

So late each night Matt would come to her room, as his was now too much of a risk, and they would make love and lie in each other's arms until morning.

He slipped off to his own room at dawn, and Cara would sleep for a couple more hours before getting up herself. She breakfasted in the company of the Hilliers, with whom she had become firm friends - they had invited her to visit them in Surrey - and the three of them set off to the cricket together.

A week of sheer joy. A week of being thrust into a world she had never experienced.

"I've always thought cricket whites look very dashing on a man," Mrs Hillier said to Cara one day at the play. Cara privately agreed but did not dare say so. She would never have considered it were it not for her awareness of Matt's rippling bronzed muscles beneath his white shirt.

Mrs Hillier had asked Cara about her own romantic situation and Cara had told her the truth, that she was recently single and concentrating on her studies for the time being.

It was more or less the truth, anyway. Cara was trying not to give anything away: her crashing disappointment when Matt was finally caught out. Her use of the field glasses to view him when he was fielding, rather than the action on the ground. Her heightened tension when he was opening the second innings.

She tried to keep her reactions neutral but it was hard. Her connection with him brought her into the game, it made everything far more charged.

It didn't help that Matt was one of the players that Mr Hillier particularly admired, and frequently praised. She just hoped nothing showed on her face when Mr Hillier yet again lauded Matt's "outstanding performance" and "aggressive strokes".

* * *

Matt was so fired up after scoring another half century in his second innings that Cara had barely let him through the door before he was all over her. Hungry to celebrate, hungry for release he practically ripped her clothes off and threw her on the bed.

She was happy to reciprocate: the hours of waiting for him, thinking about him, had driven her nearly wild.

She couldn't believe how hard he was or how much stamina he still had after such a long day.

"I needed that so much," he said afterwards. "I needed you. I can't get enough of you."

Cara knew he was just saying it. It was just the kind of thing that people said in these circumstances, so she supposed anyway. But a tiny part of her thrilled in the hope that it was true.

She said nothing but lay there, just enjoying being with him. They were both damp and glistening with perspiration and she decided to take a shower to cool off. She would probably sleep better afterwards.

"Can I join you?" Matt asked.

His intentions were certainly not to save water by sharing the shower. The minute they were under the water he took full charge. He ran the soap all over Cara's body, paying attention to every part. His hands glided over her breasts, across her stomach, around her buttocks.

She was drowning in the water, drowning in him.

Despite his previous exertions finishing just minutes before, he was rock hard and ready for action again. Putting her hands on his body, feeling the muscles of his chest and the hard flat stomach, Cara ran her lips down his body until she was on her knees below him.

Holding him in one hand she took him in her mouth, her lips enclosing his swollen head. She wanted to be intimate with every part of him. He had given her body so much pleasure, leaving her helpless with desire so many times, and she wanted to feel the same power over him.

Matt groaned and jerked his hips involuntarily when her mouth came down on him. She felt warm and wet around him. Instead of letting him slip out when he staggered backwards against the shower wall she moved over him more firmly, taking him deeper, not letting him go.

Not that he wanted her to let go. The pressure of her hands and mouth, the sensation of her tongue swirling around him, were a rare ecstasy.

Just watching her drove him wild, that she would do this for him. That she seemed to want to do it so badly.

Her eyes were closed and she was totally focused on him, on his sensation, on his pleasure.

He found himself twisting his fingers through her hair, falling in dark, wet tendrils as the shower rained down on her.

Cara could feel him tensing. When she flicked her tongue in a certain way he would throb in her grasp. His reactions made her ache as well, she felt as though she was becoming as swollen and sensitive as he was.

She was determined not to stop. She wanted to do this all the way, to lose herself in stimulating his desire.

Her mouth kept up the pressure and Matt began to rock into her gently, not wanting go too deep, but wanting more of her. He held her head at just the angle he liked, which she seemed instinctively to accommodate.

"God I want you," he said. "It's never felt this good."

In response Cara increased the pressure, gripped him a little harder. Let the rhythm get faster.

She felt him swell. Felt the tempo build as he guided her. He was pushing into her a little deeper now, not enough to cause her discomfort, but enough that she realised he was getting to the point of losing control.

Matt had his own eyes closed now, he could only feel. His entire hardness was trapped in a hot, sweet ecstasy. She had him in complete control.

He could feel his orgasm boiling within himself. He knew he was going to come violently, long and intensely. He didn't want to choke her.

Just as he reached the point of no return she swirled her tongue around his tip one more time, right on the most sensitive nerve endings.

There was no going back.

That sweet, sharp edge...

He jerked, pulled out of her, but couldn't get away quickly enough and his seed spilled out over her face, each pulse carried in rivulets by the water, down her body and away.

Cara was still holding him, looking up at him. Her own eyes were glazed with desire.

He wanted to bury himself in her.

He scooped her up, laid her on the bed and forcefully pulled her legs apart. She was clean and dripping wet from the shower, yet when he inserted a finger in her he could feel her own slick moisture.

Knowing he needed some recovery time - probably considerable after the violence of the orgasm he had just had - he wanted to make this all about her. He gripped her hips, pulling her against his face.

It was usually something Matt could take or leave. But with this girl he desperately wanted to feel her trembling with need as he focused his attentions on her.

Something about her - being younger than him, being less experienced than him - turned him on. He had been her first and he felt an unsettling sense of male pride wanting to also be the best. As though he were in competition with an unknown future lover of hers.

"Want me to keep going?" he asked her, deliberately tormenting her by stopping just as he could hear her breathing getting shallower and her body starting to spasm.

"Yes, oh god, please don't stop." Cara felt ashamed of her own wantonness: she still struggled to articulate her needs, but he was driving her wild.

Matt was loving the power he had over her. He was feeling both possessive and territorial. Even the thought of her ex fiancé pissed him off and spurred him on to make her completely lose control under his ministrations.

"There?" he demanded. "Or there? Do you want me to do this?"

"Yes, everything. Everywhere." She was just a rush of sensations, wherever he touched her was driving her wild. All her nerves were jangled together, when he touched her between her legs she felt it throb to her nipples. Her body was completely connected in sheer craving for his touch.

He was using his fingers now so he could continue to talk to her. He could feel himself starting to go hard again as well.

"Like this?" He would circle her most sensitive spot, then withdraw. Curl his fingers inside her. Stretch her. Pull her tender folds.

Enough to cause her just a bit of discomfort, to make her writhe a little more beneath him. So she would know he was in charge. So when he gave her pleasure, it was all the more heightened.

"And this?"

"Please." She was practically begging him now. Every thing he did to her was a sweet, unending agony of desire.

Sensing she couldn't take much more and knowing he was going to need release again himself, he spread her taut with his hands and put his mouth straight over her bud. He sucked on her forcefully.

It was just what she needed. She actually screamed and writhed when she came, wanting him to stop as it was suddenly too intense, but he kept going, draining her of every last wave and shudder of pleasure.

Then he moved up her body, and kissing her gently, he slid inside her and slowly, slowly began to take his own pleasures from her yet again. He could do this all night.

9. Last day of play

When Cara awoke that morning she found herself still in Matt's arms. Startled, she looked at the alarm clock and saw that it was already well into the morning. Still early, but she was used to him leaving at dawn.

She woke him, expecting him to be in a state of panic at the time but he opened his eyes and gave her a lazy smile.

"Won't you be late?" she asked anxious.

"I'll be fine." He took a lightning fast shower to refresh himself and Cara tried not to overly stare at his bronzed body as he emerged with nothing but a small white hand towel around his hips.

He pulled his previous night's clothes on and bent over the bed to kiss her goodbye.

"I did wake at dawn, actually, but I didn't feel like leaving."

Before she could react he had left her and gone off to join his team mates.

Cara sat there, the sheet still swirled around her, wondering what to make of it all. She felt she was treading a dangerously fine line. She didn't have Matt's experience, his worldliness that made it easy for him to keep things casual. Or so she thought it must be for him.

It was time for breakfast. The Hilliers would distract her from her thoughts.

"Good morning dear, I hope you slept well?" Mrs Hillier said as Cara joined them at their table. She had worried about intruding on so much of their time, but they were the ones that kept inviting her to share their company.

Cara hadn't slept very much at all due to Matt's attentions, and hoped it didn't show.

"Quite well thank you." She could hardly tell them the truth.

"The last day of play. We've been lucky to have such an exciting game, there's still everything to play for," Mr Hillier said.

Cara wasn't anticipating the same level of excitement as before since Matt was no longer batting. England would be fielding that day, hoping to capture enough Sri Lankan wickets in time for victory. Matt's amazing performances had put England in a strong position, but anything could happen on the day.

Yet she was still gripped, all the more so when Matt caught out one of the Sri Lankan opening batsmen early on. It put the England team into a winning mindset, dashed the hopes of the home side, and saw the wickets "fall like ninepins", as Mr Hillier put it. The Sri Lankans were all out shortly after lunch, and England took the victory.

Not having expected she would suddenly have a free afternoon due to the play ending early, Cara was at a momentary loss of what to do. Going to the beach was the most obvious option. She could top up her tan before flying home the next day.

They would all be leaving tomorrow: Matt and the team for another city in Sri Lanka, and Cara back to England. Matt had tried to persuade her to extend her trip but they both knew it was impossible. Things were risky enough as it was. It would be greatly pushing their luck to spend two more weeks together, only to have to part anyway at the end of the tour.

Matt insisted on taking one chance though: there was a party that night - which would now be a very celebratory one - and he wanted Cara there. "Even if you can't come as my personal guest I can still talk to you," he said.

Cara doubted that he would be able to spend much time with her at all. He'd have to do the rounds and speak to endless people as the victorious captain and also Man of the Match. But it was her last night and spending it by herself or going to bed early and reading did seem a waste. Besides, she knew some of the other players to speak to so she wouldn't be standing there like a wallflower.

* * *

Lying on the beach later that day Cara felt like a very different person to the heartbroken, inexperienced girl who had arrived a week earlier. Yet she knew she was going to be heartbroken again. There were no two ways about it: she had fallen for Matt Curran, and she had fallen hard.

It was inevitable, she supposed. He was her first real lover, even if it was supposed to be only about her body and not her heart. Being on an idyllic tropical island just helped stir up the romance even further.

She thought about her plans for the party that evening. The old Cara would have put on a simple sundress, demure rather than revealing, and spent the night talking shyly to people like the Hilliers, before turning in early and alone.

The new Cara had different plans. She'd seen an outrageously sexy gown in a boutique near the hotel and had decided to buy it. She had spent so little money on her trip, due to spending all her days at the cricket with free tickets, that she could more than afford to treat herself.

It was a sheer wisp of midnight blue silk, one-shouldered to show off her tanned skin. It skimmed her body, flowing over her curves and making her feel sinuous and alluring.

She paired it with strappy, metallic flats, not wanting to risk stumbling in heels particularly as her nerves were on edge at the thought of interacting with Matt publicly.

She left her hair loose, letting it tumble down in waves. The sun had woven gleaming colours into it: a glow of dark gold, strands of copper.

Looking at herself in the glass before she went down, she thought that her friends back home would hardly recognise her. She hardly recognised herself. How was it possible to change so much within a single week? For the world to change so much?

The mood was absolutely jubilant at the party downstairs. England had started the series on the front foot, the Sri Lankans would now have to play catch up even to draw the series.

Cara entered the room feeling rather as though she was in a dream world. She was instantly surrounded by some of the celebrating players, pressing drinks on her and chatting her up. Jeremy, whom she'd spoken to just once since the earlier party, was particularly friendly.

More than just friendly, he was clearly planning to make a move. Hoping that he would be drunk enough not to really mind when she turned him down, Cara allowed him to flirt with her a bit. She told herself she was doing it to be polite, but really she was hoping to see if it would get a reaction out of someone.

"You look as sexy as hell in that dress," Jeremy said. "Where have you been hiding all week?"

"I've been busy watching you all beat the poor Sri Lankans," she told him.

"Really? I didn't pick you for a cricket fan. Though thinking about how you put up with our captain the other night..."

He meant the first night when Matt had kissed her in the sea but Cara still got a jolt, thinking about their close shave in Matt's room the other night. Mortified, she tried to get the conversation back on track. "It's the first time I've seen a test match. Someone was kind enough to give me tickets." She thought she could imply it was the Hilliers if Jeremy probed.

But Jeremy had no plans to leave his line of commentary. He was a bit resentful that Matt had managed to get in first with Cara, as he'd been the one who invited her to the previous party in the first place.

"He's supposed to be practically married."

He was looking at her, digging to find out how far it had gone. Cara tried once more to play it down.

"I think everyone was in rather high spirits that night," she said.

"He knew what he was doing. Still, can't say I blame him..."

His fingers had found their way to the small of Cara's back, fondling the silk of her dress.

Before Cara could start to extricate herself from what was going to be an obvious move, their conversation was interrupted.

There he was.

Matt.

Looking absolutely devastating in a white linen shirt that reminded her of his cricket clothes.

And absolutely furious.

"Jeremy." He nodded to his team mate, but he didn't smile. He turned to Cara.

"Good to see you here. Did you manage to see any of the cricket this week?"

His distance was flawless. She might have been nothing but a business acquaintance that he had only met once before.

Inside Cara was confused and devastated, though she told herself he was putting on a necessary act.

But it hurt. It reminded her that after this week, they would be strangers again.

"I did, yes." What should she say? That it was very enjoyable? What was the polite convention for telling someone that you had admired their sporting performance?

"Did you enjoy it?"

"Yes, very much." She saw the merest flicker in his eye as she responded. Despite his intended reserve, Matt couldn't prevent a few images of Cara enjoying his more personal performances from coming into his head.

Jeremy had dropped his hand from her back after Matt's arrival. Cara used the opportunity to inch away from him a little. This naturally brought her closer to Matt. She didn't want to give anything away, but she really didn't want the other cricketer pawing her. He was probably a nice young man, but she simply wasn't interested. Even without Matt he wouldn't have been her type.

"Looks like you could use another drink," Matt said, indicating Cara's nearly empty glass. She was already drinking more than she meant to due to her heightened nerves. "Do the honours, Jeremy?" He held out his own glass as well. His tone was civil but was a command, not a request, and both men knew it.

Reluctantly Jeremy went off to the bar to get a fresh round of drinks, and Matt was left alone with Cara.

"I know I need to be discreet," he said in a tone low enough that no one else would have been able to hear it. "But if I see him put his hands on you again, he's out of here."

Cara was disturbed and thrilled by his possessiveness. Or protectiveness?

"It really is alright, I don't think he meant anything by it," she said to reassure him.

"Didn't he?"

"We were just talking." She avoided saying what the subject of conversation had been, given it had been Matt.

Matt raised his eyebrows. "Every man in the place is eyeing you up in that dress. I don't imagine they want merely to talk." His tone was unfairly accusatory, she thought.

"It's just a dress. I'm hardly wearing a sign that says grope me."

Matt swore. "I'm sorry. You're right, of course it's not your fault. And you look absolutely beautiful," he said, lowering his voice further.

Cara felt joy and relief. "Really?"

"You must know that you do. You're easily the most beautiful girl in the entire place. It's driving me crazy that I have to pretend to barely know you."

She was happy now. "You'd better move on then, or we'll have been talking too long."

"OK. But go and talk to someone else yourself, not that idiot. Will I see you tonight?" he asked quickly, just as the aforementioned idiot returned with their drinks.

"You know where I'll be. Probably…" she said to tease him.

"Before midnight."

He left, and Cara wondered how she would get through the next few hours since now all she could think about was her final night with him.

She was the toast of the party in her blue silk dress, surrounded by admiring males all evening. Women were outnumbered anyway, particularly when it came to young, single women.

It was a surreal experience. She didn't have to buy a single drink for herself and tried not to feel guilty since she had no intention of taking up any of the various advances made to her.

She caught Matt's eye a few times - they had to be careful - but it was like a cord connected them together across the room. At times she felt as though no one else existed there except her and him. Everyone else was blurred and indistinct.

Yet the attention was flattering and exciting. She felt adrenalin, she glowed. She found it easy to talk to people, her usual reserve melted away.

Watching her across the crowd had caused Matt to grit his teeth against the surges of jealousy he felt. He tried to reason with himself. He had no claim on her, after all. What was it to him if some other guy was chatting her up?

But it rankled. She had been this shy, sweet thing that was his discovery. Now suddenly she was the girl of the night. If he had been officially with her, openly, he would have felt proud. As it was he felt denied, robbed of something.

10. Final night

Matt had meant to avoid alcohol as much as possible, but he'd had at least a couple more than he intended to just because he was so frustrated with the events of the party. He was also frustrated with himself: why on earth was he letting this girl get to him?

It had irked him in a quite an alarming way to see other men flirt with her. It wasn't as though he was ever going to see her again after tomorrow, so why should he care?

The only thing that had made it bearable, watching some of his teammates chatting her up, was knowing that he was going to be the one spending the night with her.

He finally saw her slip away. From then on he just felt like he was counting down the minutes until he could get away himself and join her.

Most of the other party goers were too merry with drink and celebration to notice Matt's own mood. He could quite rightfully claim exhaustion, and as captain he wasn't expected to party to the bitter end. The opposite in fact.

Letting a couple of people know he was turning in for the night - in case someone went looking for him - he exited the party and caught the lift to Cara's floor.

She opened the door to him, still in the slinky blue dress. It simultaneously made him want to rip it off her so he could finally devour the tanned curves beneath, to have them all for himself, and it also enraged him because he recalled the other men's reactions to her in it.

Cara saw the dark expression on his face though she didn't fully understand it. It was as though a storm was passing over him, a black mood.

There was no gentleness now, no slow seduction.

He took a step towards her.

"I want to fuck you senseless."

Then his hands were gripping her shoulders, so hard she could feel it would leave marks on her skin, and his mouth came hard down on hers. He was crushing her, punishing her for his own frustrations and inner conflict.

Her first reaction was a surge of desire at his touch and the taste and smell of him: cologne, sweat, cigarette smoke from the bar, a trace of alcohol on his breath. Raw, utterly male.

Even as her body reacted to him her mind was confused, and she tried to wrest herself from his grasp.

As she struggled, Matt cupped a hand over her buttocks and brought her firmly against him, forcing his legs between hers so she was pressed against him. She could feel his hardness though his clothes.

Cara wanted him badly but why did he seem so angry?

He pushed her against the wall, pinning her against it with his body.

"I need this from you, I've needed it all damn night."

He kissed her down her neck, hard, biting her skin. She felt the cold, solid surface of the wall behind her. Cool against her back, where the bare skin of her shoulders was pressed against it.

Then the heat of his mouth on her chest. The heat of his hands, moulding her to him.

He seemed to want to consume her.

Then he picked her up and threw her on the bed, ripping off his own shirt as he did so.

He peeled her dress down - she was bra-less beneath it - and his hands and mouth went over her breasts. She felt like his plaything but she arched her back into his grasp, wanting to deepen the sensation as he played with her nipples.

Matt tugged the dress fully off her. Even more roughly he pulled her underwear down.

Then she heard him pull the rest of his clothes off, the clink of his belt as it slipped to the floor.

For some reason she tried to sit up, as his hands had momentarily released her. But as soon as she raised her body he pushed her back down, his hands on her shoulders.

Cara had closed her legs as he lay her on the bed, but now he moved them apart forcefully. She wanted to tell him that she was ready, willing, but something about his intensity thrilled her. He wanted her to feel that he was in command, that he wasn't giving her a choice, so she let him do so.

His knees pushing her thighs apart, he gripped her wrists and held them above her head. It lifted her breasts higher, and Matt kissed the underside before his tongue swirled over the taut peaks.

He was rock hard. He had never felt this turned on nor this frustrated.

She lay there, her hair spilling over the pillow, her eyes softened with wanting him. But there was uncertainty there too. She was both fascinated and frightened by his aggression.

The image of Jeremy pawing her flared up briefly in Matt's mind, and furious, he drove straight into her.

To blot out any other men in her life.

To make her his.

She cried out as he entered her fast and hard, but he couldn't hold back. He needed this so badly.

Cara could do nothing but take him. He still held her wrists. He was deep inside her, with each thrust it was nearly uncomfortable but she twisted her hips to match his rhythm, grinding against him.

He lowered his body over hers, his chest against hers. He buried his face in her neck and fucked her so hard she was whimpering.

He was saying something she couldn't make out. She didn't know if it was about her or something else. It was hard to think because her body was so overrun by him that it drowned out everything else.

Her wrists were painful where he was gripping her and she longed to touch him, to feel the powerful muscles of his back, his buttocks, to guide him rocking into her.

Yet her powerlessness made her feel liquid inside.

Then Matt was looking at her, directly into her eyes as he plunged into her. "I want you to come for me, now. I want to feel you come while I fuck you."

He was demanding dominion over her body.

"Now, Cara. Come for me."

She acquiesced.

It overtook her, that sweet, intense feeling. Building through her body as she writhed underneath him.

He still refused to let her escape his grasp. Her body was stretched out beneath him which made everything more intense.

Cara was completely exposed to him. Her body, her mind, completely subjugated by him.

Matt was reaching his own orgasm too. It was more violent that he ever remembered. It seemed to go on forever and all he could think about was how amazing this girl felt, how she seemed to wring every last sensation and energy out of him as she climaxed.

The simultaneousness of it. The way they were one single flesh.

Exactly together. Exactly right.

Despite his fitness he was absolutely drained. He stayed inside her, collapsed on her.

His weight crushed her. She felt faint from everything. He had finally loosened her hands and she was able to put them around him, holding his back.

She thought he had fallen asleep but then he shifted and moved his head to look at her.

"This isn't what I planned," he said.

"What isn't?"

"You. Everything."

Then his lips were on hers and it was tender, sensuous. Compared to the way he had bruised them before it was as though he was healing them.

He raised his head again, once more meeting her gaze. There was a different light in his eyes now.

Despite what he had done to her, the brink he had brought her to and beyond, he looked resigned. As though there had been a battle, which he hadn't won.

* * *

Cara slept for a while until something awoke her. Matt was resting on his elbow, looking down at her in the semi-darkness. Moonlight and other lights from outside cast some illumination into the room.

He brushed a strand of hair from her face.

"Did I hurt you before?" he asked.

He had, but far less than the pleasure he had brought her. "No, it was wonderful for me."

He looked relieved.

"I didn't mean to take it out on you. I was frustrated with…. things."

He didn't specify what and she couldn't guess. Something to do with his team perhaps.

"You are such an incredible girl. I wish circumstances could have been different," he said. He wished they were different. He was starting to wonder whether they could be.

It was the enormity of it though. To create that much disruption for what was just supposed to be a fling. If she wasn't lying there right now, looking so perfect and so sexy, if he was away from her and had his head together, he wouldn't even be considering the things that his mind was currently toying with.

Cara had no idea what thoughts were running through Matt's head. He had been straight with her at the start so she had no expectations. She had occasional wild fantasies of what could have been, if things were different, but she knew it was over tomorrow. And it was already tomorrow: past midnight.

She felt strangely at peace with it all, lying there with him. It had been perfect, for her anyway, and she could pack it up in her mind and her heart and treasure it. She had accepted that she was going to go home and her current happiness would come crashing down, but she would bear it.

She was grateful. He had opened her world to something other than Declan. There wasn't even pain there anymore, just a shuddering sense of relief that she had been saved from what would have been a miserable marriage. At least she now knew what was out there.

The question of whether she would ever find it again, whether anyone could move her world as Matt had, she buried deep down for now.

"It's been the most amazing week for me, truly," she said. "I never knew cricket could be so exciting." She was teasing him but it was true. She had actually enjoyed the cricket enormously, though it paled in comparison to Matt's off-pitch performance.

"Just the cricket?" he asked.

"What else?"

"How about this?" He trailed his finger around her breast in a spiral, reaching the bud of her nipple and playing with it gently until it peaked.

"Or this?" His other hand slipped between her legs and ran gently up gently up through her folds, to just near her nub that was electric whenever he brushed it. She longed for him to touch her there but forced herself to keep still.

"No, the cricket was still the best," she said.

"What about this then?" His mouth went over her breast, sucking with just the pressure he had learned was perfect for her. Meanwhile his finger swirled more closely around her most sensitive spot.

Cara squirmed with pleasure.

Matt loved that she was struggling to maintain her self-control. That he could play her body like this, so easily.

"If it's no good I can stop," he said, and did.

Cara's whole body ached with disappointment. But he was going to make her beg for it.

"That was possibly as good as the cricket," she told him. "Maybe you should try again."

"Which part?" He teased her nipple, with his fingers then his tongue, then pressed directly on her button.

She gasped. "That. All of it. Please don't stop this time." She was pleading with him now.

Matt couldn't remember anyone wanting him this badly and it was a huge turn on. Looking at her, completely open to him and wanting him, he felt a strange tenderness. He wanted to make love to this girl. Even if it was the last time, their last night, he wanted to rejoice in her body as though there was nothing else tomorrow.

"I want you to tell me what you want. I want this to be perfect for you," he said.

Cara didn't know what to ask for. Everything he did to her felt perfect.

"Just for you to be inside me again."

It was what Matt wanted too, but this time he entered her slowly, gently. He wanted to draw this out. To savour every sensation of how she felt around him: tight, warm, wet.

To feel her body below him, the soft swells and curves. To taste her skin.

He felt a connection with her. Their bodies matched perfectly. And he felt that she understood him. That she would have wanted him even if he hadn't been who he was.

Matt was so used to girls lusting after his fame, his celebrity. In the early days it was an ego boost, but later on it became the reverse. You couldn't tell if someone was faking it - desire, attraction, liking - just to get the glory of being with someone famous.

Cara hadn't even known who he was. Nor had she seemed any more excited or into him when she had realised. She had been worried, embarrassed, if anything, at the knowledge.

With her there were no pretences. Just two people, close, intimate.

He was moving in and out of her deeply, slowly, gently.

Her body was on fire, tingling all over. Her eyes were closed and she was smiling, her hands twisting his hair, caressing his back.

Matt knew it was madness, but he couldn't bear never experiencing this again.

"Maybe we should catch up again, back in England?"

She just felt too good to let go. He didn't know what he was saying or even what he intended. Maybe they could continue the fling back home. Maybe he could do the unthinkable.

Her eyes opened, startled. "But you said…"

"I know. It's all a mess. It's just this… you… it's felt really good." She'd been good for his game too. He had been calmer, more centred. More focused. Which was usually the opposite of what a relationship did to his sporting performance.

He dug his arms around her and rolled onto his back with her on top, keeping inside her. He loved how she felt on top of him, where he could guide her hips, feel the sweet pressure of him on his body.

"Hasn't it felt great for you too?" he asked her.

"Of course." But she didn't have anything to compare it to. The thought that she might have felt better to him than the average girl, that this felt special to him in some way, filled her with a strange terror and joy.

"You don't want a repeat performance?"

She laughed, even as he made her catch her breath as he deliberately twisted his hips and ground against her more closely.

"Yes, but…"

The but was everything. They both knew that. It was the fact he wasn't free. It was the fact that they led completely different lives. It was the fact that if they were found out it would be front page news.

Still, Matt couldn't just let her walk away. "But you'll think about it?"

She looked serious for a moment. "If you think that's what you want, then yes."

It was enough for now. Right now he was getting harder and hungrier for her.

He rolled her onto her back again, and let her know it.

11. Parting

Cara woke up in Matt's arms the next morning for the final time.

He was already awake, watching her. "Good morning." Then he kissed her, and made love to her slowly and languidly. For once they actually had some time, as she didn't need to leave the hotel until mid-morning and his flight was later in the afternoon.

"I'm going to miss this," he told her. "It will be your fault if my game suffers."

Cara laughed. "Are you superstitious?"

"No. But you've been good for me."

Good for more than just his game though. For his peace of mind. For his happiness.

Cara didn't believe him about his game. After all he was a professional sportsman. But it was nice that he said it.

He showered with her. She loved the feel of his hands over her body, underneath the running water. They only kissed this time but it felt perfect.

She tried to commit his body to memory. She closed her eyes, trying to remember the shape and feel of his chest, arms and shoulders with her hands.

Matt turned her round to face the shower wall and ran his fingers over her shoulder blades and down her back. He cupped her buttocks, massaging them with his thumbs. He had such strong, firm hands.

Cara could feel the effect he was already having on her body, yet again.

"One more time. Then I'll let you go, I promise," he said.

"I'll miss my flight."

"You won't. I'll drive you to the airport myself if you need."

She relaxed, and let him work her legs apart. It was strange not facing him, trusting him. His hands came around her front, over her lower stomach, and she arched her back. It pushed her rear back against his groin.

Then his hands slid down and he managed to position himself between her legs, Parting them slightly he thrust forwards and upwards.

They were joined. It was the most incredible feeling. Matt rocked in and out of her, savouring the way she felt.

But he needed to get them both there quickly, so his hand slipped to her front, his finger circling directly around her nub.

"You know that I'd want to go all day if I could," he told her.

The double stimulation of having him inside her and pressing her so directly in front as well was bringing Cara to the edge very quickly. It was making her writhe against Matt, which in turn was taking him to the point of losing it.

She was such a perfect fit. So tight, so sweet, so perfectly matching his rhythm.

He loved it when she came, knowing that he was the one able to give her such pleasure. It wasn't something he had thought about much before. Of course he wanted to satisfy his partners, but with Cara it was something else. He wanted to be generous.

When she came, almost losing her balance from the force of it, he felt a surge of tenderness. Her orgasms always triggered his as her contractions rippled over him.

Then as they eased apart the shower washed everything away. He wanted to just hold her there a while longer, with the water falling on them like hot rain.

He turned her back to him and kissed her, his tongue sliding inside her mouth, water running down their faces. She clung to him for a moment and then they both had to get ready for their respective days.

"I hope it goes well. The rest of the series," Cara said as they dried themselves off with the hotel towels. She meant him, of course. She would be happy if England won, for his sake, but it didn't really matter to her either way so long as Matt did okay.

"So long as the boys keep it together, we'll be fine." And if he did, of course. He had been seriously distracted this week but it hadn't done him any harm. There was nearly a week between this test finishing and the next starting. Such a waste that his distractions couldn't continue…

Cara had done most of her packing the previous evening before the party. She only had to pull on jeans and a comfortable top for travelling. It was a long journey to the airport and then twelve hours in the air. She wasn't looking forward to it.

Matt wanted to help take her suitcase downstairs, but they still had to be discreet. So she called a porter and Matt hid out of sight until he had gone.

"I really wish you were coming on the rest of the tour," he said.

The sincerity in his eyes made her wish she could manage it somehow, but it wasn't possible with her studies. And the risk of them being caught would simply escalate.

He kissed her. For the last time, before she left him. "I will call you when I'm back in England. I promise. I meant what I said last night, I want to see you again."

Cara's heart fluttered with hope but at the back of her mind she knew that people said these things and didn't follow through. He had nearly a month left on tour, anything could happen. He also had a girlfriend waiting for him back home.

So she smiled, and kissed him back one final time and went. She knew she would be a blur of tears once her taxi left the hotel, but for now she would maintain her self control.

* * *

Matt lingered in Cara's room, now empty, before returning to his own. Having spent so much time with her over the past week his schedule now seemed very empty.

Actually he would be busier than ever. There were various official events for him to attend, plus team meetings, training and of course the test matches. He would throw himself into it all, distract himself.

It felt like the colour had gone out of the sun but maybe that was just the sky, it was a hazy morning.

He had only just showered but now he needed a cold shower. He also needed to find out if his intention to look her up in the UK was something he merely felt in the heat of the moment. Right now the desire to see her again was so strong he wanted to grab a cab to the airport that minute, and race her to the plane.

So he kept himself busy. He packed his gear. Made some training notes. He had a perfunctory phone conversation with Miggy. He should have felt guilty, he supposed, but he didn't. The two women were from completely separate worlds.

Or perhaps two separate times. He felt more guilty that he didn't feel particularly excited about seeing Miggy again. In fact he wasn't sure if he could see a future with her anymore. Had he ever done?

Regardless of whether he ever saw Cara again, his time with her had reminded him again what a relationship could feel like. Should feel like.

Relationship? Was he really thinking in those terms? It had been just a fling after all, he told himself firmly.

Yet he couldn't stop the occasional misgivings when he thought of Cara. The spectre of her ex fiancé loomed in his mind. Declan. He sounded like such a tosser. What if he was back on the scene, contrite? Trying to win her back?

Thinking about it annoyed him so much he had to force it from his mind.

It was time to concentrate on his game. On his career. Something he probably should have been doing all along.

* * *

Cara had bought a thick novel from the airport for her flight back, but she couldn't even get through the first page. Her mind was whirling, replaying everything.

Some years ago she had kept a diary and she rather wished she had one now, as she had found it cathartic. But this wasn't the kind of thing you could commit to paper. Thoughts swirled around: they were more colours and feelings and impressions than something you could lock down into phrases and sentences.

For now she was in limbo. That was the only way to describe it. If they had just ended it then and there, as planned, she could have flown home, got on with her life. Maybe cried and eaten chocolate a few times. But she could have moved on.

Now she faced an agonising wait. He might only be on tour for another three weeks, but there were no guarantees that he would call her straight away.

And of course he might well change his mind. On balance Cara thought that this was most likely.

She toyed with her book. The cover showed some couple embracing in a torrid fashion with the sea behind them and a full moon above them. The man appeared to be dressed as some kind of pirate.

Cara hadn't even really studied the book before buying it, she had just grabbed the first trashy looking novel available. There was something just slightly reminiscent of their first night together about the cover. Though she had of course been wearing a bikini rather than a flowing velvet gown with her breasts heaving above a dishevelled corset.

"Tea or coffee?" The stewardess had reached her row with the drinks trolley.

Cara chose tea. She put the slice of lemon offered to her in it, watching the brown turn to a yellow gold from the acid.

She had a window seat but it was over the wing and there were only clouds outside. The plane was carrying her further and further away from Matt. Back to reality.

12. Time apart

"Nothing happened with you and that girl, did it?"

Matt was so startled by the question that he nearly knocked his beer over.

Chris, a fast bowler and one of his closest mates on the team, was looking at him intently. They were having a drink after arriving at the hotel ahead of the second test.

Matt played for time. "What on earth makes you ask that?"

"Everyone saw what happened that first night, there was a bit of talk in the dressing room. You've been AWOL all week." Chris hesitated. "Jaffo's been stirring it up a bit as well."

Jeremy Afford. Matt felt like wringing his neck. "What's he saying?"

"That you elbowed him out of the way at the party the other night, when he was talking to her. The same girl."

Right at that moment Matt wished he'd punched Jeremy's lights out. Perhaps he still would.

"Next time you publish the social diary, you can put any rumours to rest. As you know, I've got a girlfriend," he said.

"Everyone does know. That's why there was talk," Chris told him. "Let's face it, she was pretty stunning. No one could blame you."

Damn them all. Things were complicated enough without this. Matt felt defensive. And once again annoyed at other men leering over Cara.

"I barely spoke to her." He kept his tone neutral and hoped he sounded convincing. "I don't know what you mean by AWOL either. I've been out with the rest of you every night." He knew he had nearly always been the earliest to leave, but that wasn't unexpected for a captain. He wasn't supposed to be drinking until dawn.

"More a state of mind. You've been distant." Chris called for another round of drinks. "If there is something the matter and you need an ear, well, you know I owe you one. More than one."

There was genuine concern in Chris's face. Matt had been there for him when his marriage broke down a couple of years ago. Bringing round takeaways every night, dragging him out to the pub so he didn't drown his sorrows alone. Since Matt had met Miggy they'd seen less of one another, except at cricket, but the bond was still there.

Chris didn't care for Miggy, he thought she seemed high maintenance and demanding, but he wanted Matt to be happy. He assumed Matt's stress was related to his high profile girlfriend in some way. He couldn't think what else could be bothering him.

"No, it's all good." Matt drained his drink and picked up the next one. He didn't meet Chris in the eye, and they both knew he was lying.

Maybe he'd unburden himself later, maybe he wouldn't, Chris thought. Either way Matt was resilient. He'd figure it out somehow, whatever it was.

"Just shut Afford up if you can. You know what it's like. I don't need something like that getting out."

So it was true then. Chris wondered if Matt realised he'd given himself away. It would be fireworks if Miggy found out.

* * *

Ann, Cara's best friend and flatmate at university, was delighted with the gemstone necklace Cara had bought her as a souvenir. Cara had finally finished unpacking and they were sitting on the sofa having coffee.

"I'm sorry I didn't send a postcard, I figured I would arrive back before it did," Cara said.

"Don't worry about that! Tell me what it was like, did you have a good time? You didn't spend all your time thinking about Declan did you?"

It was amazing how little Declan had been on her mind, when Cara thought about it. He had been the biggest thing in her life for the past couple of years, she had been planning an entire future with him, but now it all felt like something that had happened very long ago.

She didn't even feel any hurt any more, or any anger. Just relief that she had learnt what was really out there and how much better it was.

"No, I was fine. I had a lovely time." She couldn't stop memories of Matt flooding into her head as she said this. She was going to have to mention the cricket at least, as many of her photos were taken at the ground and Ann would think it was odd otherwise. "I had no idea when I booked but the England cricket team were playing there. Someone at the hotel gave me some spare tickets and I went to the match. It helped take my mind off things."

"Really? You were so devastated before you left. I felt awful not being able to come with you." Ann noticed Cara's expression. "You look all dreamy. You're not thinking of him now, are you?" She was anxious for her friend.

For a moment Cara thought Ann meant Matt. "No, something else. It's fine. I'm over him, really," Cara said. She felt her face growing red.

"Someone else, by the look on your face." It was Fiona, their third flatmate. Inexplicably wearing high heeled boots, a kimono and a face mask, she had come into the sitting room to find some papers.

Ann looked back at Cara. "Really? Already?"

"Goodness no!" Cara did everything she could to make her denial sound convincing. Ann, with her sweet and sheltered outlook on life, dating a trainee vicar, was the last person in the world to whom she could confess something like Matt.

She felt bad that there was a barrier between herself and her friend. But she remembered Matt's phrase: "What goes on tour…"

Whatever happened in future, for now she would have to keep her own counsel. Bury the secret deep down, and take each day as it came.

Fiona was not so easily put off. She accosted Cara later that evening in the kitchen when Cara came in make some tea. She was making an instant meal for herself, as cooking facilities in their tiny flat were pretty limited. Eating from a disposable plastic tray also meant less washing up.

"Something's up with you. No one gets over a broken heart that quickly, not the way you were before you left. And you've been in a strange mood since you got back."

"I just realised over there that it was all for the best. That we weren't really that well suited, and it was more the shock that upset me." Cara did her best to allay Fiona's suspicions.

"Maybe." Fiona got her food out of the microwave. She sat down at the kitchen bar to eat. "There was someone, wasn't there?"

Cara weighed up whether or not it would be wise to unburden herself to Fiona. The other girl was fairly experienced with men, she had even had an illicit liaison with one of their tutors the previous year. So she wouldn't be judgmental at least.

"Yes. There was." She decided to admit it.

"Good for you. I always say the best medicine is to get back in the saddle." Fiona grinned. "Not that I imagine Declan was much of a ride." She had considered the man a complete drip and had wondered what Cara saw in him. He was reasonably good looking, but so effete. Fiona hated fussiness in a man.

"I suppose that's for Lucinda to enjoy now," Cara said.

"More fool her. So, are you seeing him again or was it just a holiday fling?"

"I'm not sure. It's all a bit complicated." Knowing this wouldn't satisfy Fiona, who could prise a confession out of the Pope, Cara gave her a swift overview of the basic details. That the England cricket team were in the same hotel, how everyone had had too much to drink, that she'd ended up having a liaison with the England captain which had gone on all week.

Fiona was silent for a while. She studied Cara, frowning slightly. Then she picked up her fork and started eating again.

"So this did actually happen," she said through a mouthful of food. "This isn't some sort of joke or hallucination?"

"No. It almost feels that way, being back here."

"You do know he's supposed to be dating that model, Miggy Chatham?" Fiona asked.

"Of course. The first time though, I didn't realise who he was. And then…"

"…and then tropical nights and torrid passion? Throwing caution to the wind?"

"Something like that." Cara felt rather ashamed. Though it hadn't really been like that, not on her side anyway. She had genuinely liked him and enjoyed being with him. She had thought they had a connection.

She didn't dare say this because it probably made her sound pathetic. Desperate. All the more so if he never did call her, and back in the cold grey rainy reality of England she was increasingly uncertain that he ever would.

Fiona wasn't judging her though. "You know if he dumps her for you, you'll be all over the newspapers."

"I know. I'm not really expecting it to happen though," Cara said.

"If it did, it would certainly liven this place up. And I'd love to see the look on Declan's face."

Fiona stashed her now empty tray in the bin, rinsed her fork in the sink, and went off to her room.

Cara was left alone with her cup of tea. She felt flat. She missed Matt, but more than that. She felt something was missing from her life.

* * *

The second test wasn't going as well as the first. Matt had gritted his teeth and got stuck into his own game. He was battling it out and his play was robust, even if it lacked flair. But the tensions in the team between him and Jeremy, the gossip that he now knew was going on, all of it weighed on him.

Even Chris's steady presence couldn't fully assuage him. He was stressed.

Miggy was phoning frequently. The first time the phone in his new hotel room rang Matt had found himself hoping it was Cara. He'd even considered putting her name on the approved caller list with reception in case she did try to ring. But it would far too risky. If anyone got hold of it, it would be a nightmare.

So he tried to hold conversations with Miggy and not let her know there way anything wrong. Fortunately she was fairly full of her own news, and didn't pick up his changed tone. Although maybe he hadn't changed that much. He'd been tiring of the whole thing long before he met Cara.

If Miggy did comment on him sounding tired, he blamed it on the cricket. The weather. The schedule. Anything but the truth.

They lost the second test, meaning the series was neck and neck. It would make the final test more interesting for the fans if nothing else.

The team moved onto the final city and the final game, and Matt started counting down the days to getting back and sorting out his increasing mess of a personal life.

13. Flying back

It was all over the headlines as Matt flew home. There were even reporters at Heathrow when he landed.

"Matt and Miggy's baby joy!" "Curran awaits a bumper delivery." "Another bouncer for England captain!"

It was pushed in Matt's face as he left the airport. He hadn't got a clue what was going on. He gritted his teeth, attempted to maintain his composure in front of the microphones thrust towards him, and answered any cricket related questions in the usual way. For others he repeated "no comment for now" in as civil a tone as he could manage.

He was supposed to have had plenty of training for media ambushes, but he'd never anticipated something like this.

"What's happening with you then?" one of the other players asked him as they finally shook off the press pack and made their way to the taxi rank.

"Journalists, you know what they're like," Matt said. He kept his face down so he could avoid catching anyone's eye. He was in no mood to sign autographs.

As they were waiting an apologetic looking minion from the England Cricket Board rushed up to him, apologising for not being there to meet him off the plane, and handed him a celebrity magazine as he was bundled into a taxi.

"Miggy Chatham reveals her joy as she and England cricket captain fiancé Matt Curran announce they're expecting their first child. The TV presenter and fashion icon invites us into her exquisite Kensington apartment to share her excitement and baby plans, including a sneak peak at the future nursery."

Jesus Christ. Endless photos of Miggy draped over her sofa and chairs, apparently "modelling the latest collection" from some up-and-coming designer while she made coy remarks to the sycophantic reporter. Matt couldn't even bring himself to finish reading it.

"You weren't expecting her to announce it?"

Matt had had no damn clue she was expecting. "No." He was curt, but he was furious. Someone should have been able to warn him about this. This magazine interview must have been carried out days ago. Weeks, even.

"Well, congratulations of course," the minion said awkwardly. "If you'd like us to issue a statement…"

"Nothing for now, thanks."

What the hell was Miggy playing at?

He just wanted to get home, alone, to his flat, and take his phone off he hook. Because he knew it was going to be ringing all night. Even though it was unlisted the press always got hold of it.

And his parents. What the hell must they think? They would want an explanation and he didn't even have one to give them.

He was hoping it was some kind of joke. Miggy doing a publicity stunt, trying to land a new contract or something. Because anything else was just too much to stomach right now.

Matt's own mobile phone was still switched off. He would have turned it on in the taxi but there was no way he was going to do so now. Just the thought of all the voicemails piling up was enough to make him want to hurl it out of the window.

The minion's mobile rang. Looking uneasy he answered it and handed it to Matt.

Thank God it was Chris. "Your phone's off. I figured why. I'll be round at seven with a bottle of the hard stuff unless you have other plans?"

"No, all clear. Call Irene and she'll buzz you up."

Irene, an eccentric elderly artist, was Matt's neighbour. If she let Chris up it meant Matt could ignore his own intercom. He often did it as a way of screening visitors, giving Irene the occasional bottle of wine as a thank you.

What Irene really wanted was to paint him. Since Irene painted full size male nudes with what appeared to Matt to be significantly enhanced attributes, he didn't feel it was a wise move at this point in his career.

The trip from Heathrow to his flat in Regent's Park had never seemed longer. He sat there in silence, cursing every red traffic light, every jam. He wanted to be home, alone, and to lose himself in booze or sleep.

* * *

"I thought it would be fun!" was her excuse. "A lovely way to surprise you."

Matt should have guessed Miggy would be there waiting for him when he got back. They practically lived in one another's apartments when they were both in London.

He didn't believe her for a moment. She hadn't told him because she hadn't been certain of his reaction. Which was partly his fault. He'd been so distant with her the past month, while overseas.

What could he do? She was cooing over ultrasounds and he was still trying to take it all in. He could hardly be angry with her in her current state.

She didn't look any different. The same designer clothes, hair styled at one of Knightsbridge's most expensive salons earlier that day. Matt didn't have enough experience of these things to know what she was supposed to look like at this stage of pregnancy, but she seemed the same as ever.

"So aren't you excited?" She had flung her arms around him as soon as he had entered, and he'd felt forced to reciprocate.

"Of course, it's still sinking in." He really wanted some space but he could hardly ask her for it at that moment. Right now nothing seemed more desirable than Chris with a bottle of Scotch and drinking themselves to oblivion. "How have you been?"

"Great. No symptoms. That's why I didn't even realise at first, you know how irregular I am."

She had all the press clippings out on the coffee table and was criticising the photographs of herself with a professional's eye. "I told them I didn't want that photographer but it was all so last minute. Still, we'll get our choice of photographer for the wedding. Did I tell you they've offered to cover it? A hundred grand."

Wedding? They weren't even engaged.

Miggy continued her torrent of conversation. "Ma wanted it done this year, but I don't think the baby-bump bride is really me, do you? Next year will be fine. It's not as though anyone worries about that stuff these days. Some couples wait years, and have the kids as little page boys and flower girls. I think that might be a bit too much though."

"Your mother knows?"

"Yes, well I had to tell her, she would have blown a gasket if she'd read about it in the papers first. Do you know they even covered it in the Telegraph! Horrid photo of you though darling, from that charity event last August when you'd had food poisoning."

She chattered on. He interrupted her.

"You are OK with this, aren't you? I mean I know you had certain plans." Just six months ago Miggy had been adamant that she didn't plan to have children for another decade, if ever. She wanted to model, travel, try to break into Hollywood.

Matt hadn't been sure how serious she had been. A family wasn't something on his immediate calendar either, but a decade seemed a bit far ahead. Five years might have been about right.

Not that they had the luxury of choice any more.

"I can't deny it was a shock, but when life gives you lemons. Actually it is the size of a lemon right now, according to some book I got."

"Do they know when you're having it?" Matt asked.

"When it's due? The twenty-first of August. The Battle of Bosworth and Debussy's birthday. Yes, I did have to look them up, my history isn't that good. Much good will it do since the doctors are always wrong apparently. If not we might call him Claude or Claudia, if it's a she."

Bringing up gender was making it even more real for Matt. Even more enormous. He knew he should feel excited - he wanted to, he told himself - but he was just numb. He blamed it on tiredness.

"The flight was hellish, I need to take a shower."

When the water ran over him all the memories of Cara came flooding back. He could almost feel her there with him. Wildly he wished she was there. He wished they were both back in Sri Lanka, that they'd never had to leave.

But that was impossible. He was here, he had to make the best of it. He winced, thinking of Cara seeing all the headlines. She'd probably assume he'd known all along. Anyone would.

Still, at least she'd understand why he wouldn't be able to look her up. Why he couldn't see her again, ever.

He closed his eyes for a moment, drained physically and emotionally, and remembered the sweetness of her. His final fling. Miggy needn't ever know. He would do the right thing. He had no choice: he could hardly dump a pregnant girlfriend for someone else, not when he was in the public eye.

Realising this also crystallised how he had been feeling about the situation. Before all this happened he had basically decided to end things with Miggy and hopefully see Cara. He had missed her, he had dreamt of her, he had been excited at the thought of calling her and seeing her again.

All that was changed now. There was no point speculating on what might have been. And yet now it was all changed, he was starting to realise just how much it all had come to mean to him. And how little Miggy meant to him. The mother of his future child. He just couldn't take it in.

Matt felt like there was a lead weight around him. It would lift, he told himself. He'd feel better about things after a good night's sleep. Or he'd fake it until he felt it. And he would try to forget.

14. Devastation

She was devastated. She felt like a fool.

Ann had unwittingly left a copy of one of that day's newspapers on the coffee table. The very day that Matt was due back, and Cara had almost been boiling over in anticipation, literally counting the days.

When she saw the headline - stark in black and white with a photo of Matt below - she couldn't move for a moment. Or breathe.

All her perception of the future, her hopes, even her intuition that he possibly shared her feelings, had been a lie. She felt utterly betrayed.

She also knew for the first time how she really felt about him. She loved him. Matt Curran. She was in love with him: heart, body and soul.

And he was lost to her forever. Utterly, completely gone.

She had to sit down for a moment. Dazed, she couldn't even touch the paper to read it. To see if maybe there was a twist, maybe there was some other explanation.

"Matt and Miggy's baby joy!"

What other possible explanation could there be?

The shattering realisation was that he must have known. For them to announce it now, he must have known all along. All the time he had spent with her in Sri Lanka, all the things he had said, all in the knowledge that he had not just a girlfriend back home, but a pregnant girlfriend.

Eventually she managed to pick the newspaper up and actually read it. It could have been talking about any celebrity couple, the same phrasing, the same piece of information. But it wasn't about anyone: it was about Matt.

Fiona found Cara sitting there staring numbly at the wall. She hadn't responded when Fiona called hello on entering the flat. Puzzled, the other girl glanced at the newspaper that was now half sliding off the table.

"Oh god. What a complete bastard. From what you said..."

She left it hanging. They both knew what she meant.

"He was your first, wasn't he? It always hurts the worst."

Cara, through her anguish, was glad of Fiona. She understood these things. She didn't condemn.

"I had no idea. I feel so stupid."

"Don't. Men can just be total bastards when they're trying to get you in the sack." Fiona sat down by Cara in solidarity.

Not that he'd even had to try very hard, Cara thought, ashamed. She'd been cheating with someone who had a pregnant partner. Even though she may not have known, it made the whole thing seem so much worse now. So sordid.

At the time it had been elevating, like a perfect dream.

"I just thought..."

"You thought he was different? Yeah, so do we all. Every time we fall for it. But it's always the same."

"Why did he say all those things then? Why not just end it like he always planned to?" Cara asked. At least she now understood his initial insistence that it was just a fling, that it couldn't go anywhere.

Fiona shrugged. "I have no idea. Maybe he really did fall for you. Maybe he had some wild plan where he would try to be with you. If he's now thought better of it, it's for the best. You really wouldn't want to be with a man that's having a child with someone else. It's not like dating a widower with kids, or something."

"I feel so embarrassed. Like he must have been laughing at me."

Cara cast her thoughts back to the way he had looked at her. The fun they had had together. The amazing passion, every night, all night.

Fiona tried to console her.

"Some people just live in the moment. They can switch it on and off more easily than others. You probably were his world for those few days. Then out of sight, out of mind."

* * *

He was calling to her. She could see him from her balcony, on the beach, in the moonlight. He wanted her to join him. She ran downstairs and the stairs seemed to be endless. She was going to miss him. Sure enough, when she arrived on the sand, he was gone. Then she saw him in the distance. Beckoning her. She ran after him but it was too far, her feet were sinking into the sand. He was moving faster, further away than she could ever catch up with him. The moon, the stars, the vast, endless blackness of the sky... she was alone. It was too late.

Another night, another tormented dream. Cara wished she could block them out, she woke up every morning feeling worse than the night before.

Fiona's suggestion was to read a good book. "Something trashy and sexy and absorbing. Jackie Collins. Jilly Cooper. Read into the early hours until you're so exhausted you won't be able to dream." She went to the local library and picked up a stack of lurid bonkbusters for Cara.

But Cara did dream. She could have borne the pain during the daytime if she could at least have enjoyed a few hours of oblivion each night.

She was determined not to let it ruin her study though. That was all she had left now, and she wasn't foolish enough to neglect it due to heartsickness.

But she felt strangely lost. She was left with a void where previously she had a bubble of nervous hope and fear.

Ann of course knew nothing. She was perceptive enough to realise that something was up with Cara, but she put it down to delayed heartache over Declan and perhaps exam stress. After all, Cara was throwing herself into her books like never before.

She invited Cara to one of her church meetings to try and encourage her to socialise, but even if Cara hadn't felt like a scarlet woman she wouldn't have wanted to go. Ann's church was full of happily married and engaged couples and it would be salt in the wound.

Fiona had the right idea. Although Cara was reluctant, she let Fiona drag her out to a couple of nightclubs. They were places that Declan claimed to have abhorred so she had never visited them before. Now, of course, she suspected Declan's reason was actually because he took girls like Lucinda to these places and didn't want to run the risk of an awkward encounter with his unsuspecting fiancée.

Women were greatly outnumbered by men at the local club that Fiona had taken her to. The two girls weren't short of attention. Fiona was wearing one of her typically outrageous outfits: spike heeled boots, a dress with a sort of PVC corset laced over the top of it and brilliant red lipstick.

Cara wore black jeans and a low cut top that Fiona practically forced her into. "You still have a tan which no one else does in March, you may as well show it off."

The tan was fading fast. The memories less so.

By midnight Cara had heard enough "Awright, darlin'?" and "fancy a stiff one?" with the associated smirks to last a lifetime.

Fiona was apologetic. "It's a bit of a dive, isn't it? Still, he's not bad looking." She indicated a man who reminded Cara disconcertingly of Jeremy and she shuddered. Reminders everywhere.

* * *

Ann had heard on the grapevine that Declan was no longer seeing Lucinda, and told Cara thinking it would comfort her.

"It didn't last then with him and that awful girl, and I bet he hugely regrets it. Not that I think you should get back with him.

Unless you want to, of course. Whatever you decide I'll support you."

But Cara found she couldn't feel anything either way. It simply made no difference to her. She didn't even hate Declan any more, or what he had done.

There was simply nothing there. Everything was eclipsed by Matt.

But Cara had spirit. The shock had affected her badly, but she was determined to pull herself together and try to enjoy life again. So she picked herself up and forced herself to smile. She couldn't spend her last term at university moping around.

The problem was that she was so tired. She seemed to be exhausted all the time these days. Some afternoons she would get back from her tutorials and go straight to bed for a couple of hours. The good thing about this was that she did get some proper sleep: no dreams.

Ann thought she should see a doctor but Fiona knew what the truth was. "It's very draining, heartbreak. It's like a bereavement. You'll get through it."

One night Cara had been out to a party with Fiona and when she got back there was a mysterious phone message that Ann had taken.

"It was a man but he didn't leave his number. I thought it might be Declan but it didn't seem like his voice," she told Cara.

"Did he ask for me?"

"No. He just said hello, and then there was a sort of pause, and then he hung up. I thought it was for you because of Declan, but probably it was just one of Fiona's friends after a few too many drinks."

"What was his voice like?" Cara asked.

"I really couldn't say. The line wasn't great, I think he was calling from a mobile."

Cara couldn't have called Matt even if she had wanted to as she didn't have his number. He had been the one who had promised to call her.

Thinking about it, she was very fortunate the story had been splashed across the newspapers. If she hadn't known she might have tried to contact him and then been totally mortified and humiliated. It was a harsh way to find out, but as Fiona said, better to know the worst as soon as possible. And not to have heard it from him: that would be more than she could have borne.

One day she would be able to open up her box of memories, just like Great Aunt Diana, and consider them fondly. For now it was all too raw.

15. Struggling

It was an effort. A huge effort. Matt felt like he was going through the motions and his frustration grew along with his sense of guilt.

He longed to get away but England weren't touring again until the end of the year. By then he'd be a father, caught up in wedding plans, he felt like his life was spiralling out of his control.

This should be the happiest time possible for him. Career success, money, a beautiful girlfriend, a baby on the way.

Instead he felt trapped. He couldn't get Cara out of his mind as much as he tried to suppress thoughts of her.

Miggy was glowing with her pregnancy but had totally gone off sex which had been a relief to Matt rather than a frustration. Things were complicated enough as it was.

He did all the right things, or at least he tried to. He got Miggy what she wanted. He accompanied her to appointments when cricketing and captaincy duties permitted. He went window shopping for baby stuff with her.

She was planning on getting most of it for free, either through sponsorship deals or from friends and family. Miggy was never as loaded as she needed to be, but she was smart at getting things as favours. Everyone did it in her world, where you needed a new designer outfit for every event.

Matt had always admired this about Miggy: how she could charm anything out of anyone. Now he felt he would rather just pay for the damn designer pram out of pocket so they could get out of the shop and not have to endlessly look at different colours and styles.

And now he had a kid on the way, and felt a sense of duty to provide for it, it felt a bit grasping to be angling for freebies. He wasn't sure it if undermined him, somehow. If it was demeaning.

He tried talking about this with Miggy but she laughed him down. "Don't be absurd! What's the point of spending thousands of pounds on nursery furniture if someone is happy to give it to us?"

Matt attempted to explain that he wanted things to be simple. That they - and the baby - didn't need all this stuff. But Miggy mocked him for being "noble" and he ended up dropping the subject.

He should have been grateful, he supposed. He knew of enough relationships that failed under financial pressures.

Miggy also had completely different ideas about names than he had. Every day she seemed to come up with something new that he inwardly cringed at. Anoushka. Portia. Pandora. Tristram. Rollo. Cosmo. He could just imagine the reaction in the dressing room at "Cosmo Archibald Chatham-Curran", her current preferred combination.

Matt imagined something simpler. A sweet little girl called Poppy. A little boy wearing mini cricket whites called Finn. He mentioned these names to Miggy but she dismissed them as too commonplace.

If it wasn't for Chris he might have gone mad. He was a constant source of support. Although Chris hadn't had kids with his ex, he had a slew of nephews and nieces.

"It's always like this, for a first. Just ride it out."

Other team mates got on his nerves. "About time you two got hitched isn't it, before the happy arrival? When's that happening then?"

"The more people who ask the less inclined I am," Matt said. Then he felt bad for snapping, and disloyal to Miggy at the same time.

Chris could see that Matt was deeply unhappy.

One night he took him for a drink to an out-of-the-way pub, somewhere quiet that they almost certainly wouldn't see anyone they knew or be recognised. Miggy was at a pre-natal yoga class that evening, she was working hard to stay in shape, determined to "snap back" and be modelling again within weeks of the birth. She was already interviewing nannies.

Chris bought a round for him and Matt and they sat in a table tucked around the corner. That was the useful thing about old British pubs, they had nooks and crannies where you could have a drink undisturbed. Compared to the crowded and exposed meat-market of a West End club or bar.

"I'm only going to bring this up once, so hear me out," Chris said. "If you want to end it then end it. You'll deal with the fallout somehow. It won't be easy, but it's better than lying for a lifetime if you're truly in over your head."

Matt was silent for a long time. He looked at the thin stream of bubbles rising in his glass. For a moment he felt as though someone was opening a roof light, just a crack.

But it was no good. Duty was drummed into him too hard.

"I have to see this through. I have to at least try."

"It'll be different once it comes. It will reset everything," Chris said. He didn't tell Matt what he feared, that it would almost certainly change it for the worse.

* * *

When the phone rang that evening in Cara's flat and Fiona held it out to her - "it's for you" - with her eyebrows raised, Cara's stomach lurched in hope and fear.

Only to come crashing down when she heard Declan's voice at the end of the line.

There was a time when her heart would have leapt to hear him on the phone. If he had managed to call her that first afternoon in Sri Lanka, before the party and the sea ever happened, how very different things might have been.

She wouldn't have gone to the party, would never have got drunk, would never have seen Matt again.

But everything was changed now.

"I was wondering if I could come and see you?"

It was the last thing she wanted. "I really don't think so, Declan. I just don't think we have anything more to say."

"Please, I need to see you. I still have things to tell you," Declan said.

She was so tired. If she hadn't been so sapped of energy, maybe she would have refused.

"OK. But don't come round here. I'll meet you in town."

She suggested a café they both knew, it was public and neutral territory.

Fiona, who had been keenly eavesdropping, offered to come. "Moral support if you want it. And because I'll really enjoy seeing his face when you tell him where to go."

Cara thanked her but said she would be fine.

"I might just sneak down and spy on you anyway, I've got nothing else to do," Fiona said. "After having to be civil that smarmy git for months out of politeness to you, I think I deserve a bit of a show."

Cara didn't want to do herself up especially for Declan, but she wanted to look smart enough that she felt confident within herself to allay any advances he might make. The aim was to look and feel attractive and assertive. Not a pathetic broken-hearted basket-case who needed a man.

She fixed her hair, put on subtle make up, and wore a top that Fiona had given her which she'd bought in a sale and then found too tight up top.

For Cara it showed more cleavage than she would have liked but it was all part of her costume. Her armour. She even borrowed a pair of Fiona's heeled boots so she could look taller and stride in and out in a purposeful way. So she imagined, anyway.

Ann was confused as to why Cara was getting dressed up. "I thought you didn't want to impress Declan?" she asked.

"She doesn't. She wants to rub it in his face what he's missed," Fiona told her. "At least that's what I would do."

Cara still felt nervous as she entered the café. She was fifteen minutes late, at Fiona's insistence. "Let him be the one waiting around for a change. God knows how many times he kept you waiting for hours, and stood you up."

When she finally got there, Declan was sitting at a table and looked almost pathetically glad to see her. "You look amazing, Cara. I've missed you so much."

She avoided his embrace. Declan looked terrible. She wasn't sure if it was just because he looked thinner and as though he hadn't slept, or whether he had always looked like this. He also seemed shorter when he stood up to greet her, though she supposed this might have been because of Fiona's heels.

In her mind she'd always pictured him a bit like the actor Jeremy Irons: suave and artistic and very cultured. Even though he worked in insurance which was hardly any of those things.

But right now Declan just looked thin and tired and a bit weedy.

The contrast with Matt: tall, bronzed with strong arms and rippling muscles, was almost absurd.

"So what did you want to discuss?" she asked, hoping to get it over with.

"Us, of course. I've missed you more than you can imagine, what I did was sheer folly but it didn't mean anything, and I will regret it until the end of my days. All it did was make me realise we're meant to be together, Cara. Since that first time I took you out..."

Declan went on and on but Cara found herself tuning out. Her body was in the café but her mind was back in Sri Lanka. She knew that was the past, and Matt was no longer her future, but it had given her perspective. There was no way someone like Declan was going to be part of her future.

"I'm sorry, I missed what you just asked me?"

He looked annoyed and hurt. "I asked you if you would come down and visit my parents next weekend? It's been ages and they're dying to see you."

Cara burst out laughing. "Your parents? I do hope you're joking."

His parents had always treated her in a very snooty way, deliberately conveying that they didn't think she was good enough for their revered son. It had been an ordeal every time she had visited them and she had absolutely dreaded it.

"I'm not joking at all. Try to be serious. They've invited us down," he said.

Cara looked at him directly. "I am being deadly serious, Declan. There is no us. There never will be an us, it's over, forever."

Declan scowled. This meeting was not going as easily as he had anticipated. "Try not to be bitter, Cara, it's not an attractive quality."

She stood up. "I'm not bitter. I'm simply over it, over you. Flatter me, insult me, it makes no difference. I'm afraid this has been a waste of both our times."

Cara walked out of the café leaving Declan behind at the table, stunned and furious.

16. A weekend visit

A letter came for Cara the next day. It was in a thick white envelope, with her address written in beautiful, old-fashioned handwriting and a Surrey postmark. She guessed even as she opened it that it was from Mrs Hillier.

My Dear Cara, Peter and I greatly enjoyed meeting you in Sri Lanka and having the pleasure of your company at the cricket. I hope you enjoyed yourself as much as we did, and have been keeping well these past weeks. We would be delighted for you to come and spend the weekend with us at our home in Surrey if you could put up with two elderly people. Very best wishes, Evelyn Hillier.

It was an escape and a link with Matt, or at least her memories of him. Cara couldn't think of anything nicer. She rang the number included as a post script, and visions of Sri Lanka, the sunshine and the bright green pitch flooded back as she heard Mrs Hillier's voice.

"Cara, how lovely to hear from you. You received my letter? Oh, I am so glad. If it's not too soon, what about this weekend?"

They arranged that Cara should take the train to the station nearest them, and Mr Hillier would meet her there. "No need to get a taxi, my dear, we wouldn't hear of it. Do feel free to bring your work with you, I'm sure you must be very occupied with your studies, I remember how it was with our boys."

The Hilliers had three sons, who were now spread across the globe through work and marriage. It had left them rather lonely. Cara felt a slight twinge of guilt on behalf of her own family, whom she hadn't seen since Christmas. She just hadn't felt like facing anyone since the break up with Declan, and now of course her heartache over Matt. She wished she could believe it was getting better but truthfully it wasn't.

Trying to put on a false front with her family, who knew her well enough to see through most pretences anyway, seemed like too great an ordeal. But the Hilliers were different, separate. They didn't know her past and she could switch off from it at their place.

* * *

The train changed at Reading for a slow train, taking her through some of the villages fortunate enough to have escaped the worst of Dr Beeching's railway cutbacks. There was something timeless about a traditional English village with its own railway station. It took one out of the modern world, at least on a Saturday morning when the carriages were commuter-free, transporting mainly those travelling for leisure.

Mr Hillier picked her up in a very smart grey car. Cara had guessed during her time at the cricket that they were obviously well-off people. Not rich in a flamboyant way, but the kind of quiet, discreet wealth that populated this part of South East England.

He was obviously known at the station, because the stout railway porter immediately picked up Cara's bags on seeing the car and greeted Mr Hillier by name.

"I was a daily commuter before my retirement," Mr Hillier explained to Cara as he drove. "It's high time old Dennis retired but I think he prefers to keep occupied."

The Hilliers' house was called Montpellier Villa perhaps due to its white-framed French windows that opened onto level green lawns. The Hilliers were clearly keen gardeners, even though it was only March there was a carpet of spring flowers.

Mrs Hillier embraced her - "you must call me Evelyn, dear" - and ushered her in for a cup of tea. They spent the morning in reminiscences, telling Cara about the final two tests and what she had missed. Cara wouldn't usually have enjoyed endlessly talking sport but she was alert for any mention of Matt. She had of course scoured the cricket coverage in the papers since she had flown back herself, but references to him were few and far between.

She knew what he had scored, and a few quotes he had given about the game, but not how he had seemed or anything else. None of the tour gossip she had been privy to during her time over there and had been cut off from since. The Hilliers might not have enjoyed quite the intimacy with the players that Cara had, with one player at least, but they were still part of the inner crowd of England supporters.

Not that there was any point knowing any of it really. Not now. It was like grasping at the crumbs of someone else's meal.

Mr Hillier had some business to attend to at his golf club that afternoon, where he was treasurer, so after lunch Cara and Evelyn Hillier sat down together in the conservatory. Cara had assured her hostess that she didn't need to bury herself in her books straight away.

Evelyn had something of a gleam in her eye as she poured tea for them both.

"Now I'm glad we've got Peter out of the way because I know he would berate me for turning to such a subject, but men are rather dense when it comes to certain matters, aren't they?" she said.

Cara was intrigued and slightly nervous as to where this was leading.

"I must ask you, dear, even though it's absolutely none of my business, but I wondered if you perhaps had a special connection with the England team?"

Cara nearly choked on her Earl Grey.

"A connection?"

"Given you hadn't been a test cricket spectator before, and were there by yourself, and attended every day... well I'm afraid I'm probably just an inquisitive old woman with far too much time on her hands, but I did find myself putting two and two together and perhaps making five," Evelyn said. "And if so I do apologise, and really it's none of my business as I've said. I just have rather a soft spot for romance. When I first met Peter he was wearing cricket whites."

She fetched a photo down from a shelf. "This was taken a couple of years after we married, but he didn't look so different by then."

The photo showed Peter Hillier in cricket whites at what appeared to be a village match. It was black and white and depicted a really classic English scene. Cara was impressed by how handsome Mr Hillier looked and said so. Then, despite herself, her face fell.

"If I've touched on an unhappy subject, my dear, please forgive me and let's talk of other things. Peter's always telling me that I'm far too nosey and it probably is high time I heeded him," Evelyn said.

Cara saw the kindness and concern in her face. She felt so isolated herself. Fiona was the only person who knew, but she had never met Matt as the Hilliers had.

"I was involved with someone but unfortunately it didn't work out," she said.

"My dear, I am so very sorry. You seemed so very happy in Sri Lanka that I felt sure… but let's change the subject."

"It's fine, really," Cara told her. "I was very happy, but I was… misled." She couldn't think of a better way to describe it.

"He was playing the field, perhaps? An unfortunately appropriate turn of phrase for a sportsman," Evelyn said.

It was one way to put it. "Something like that." She felt guilty at accepting Evelyn's sympathy when she only had herself to blame. After all she had known he wasn't free. "To be honest I knew that there were complications, but I thought perhaps…"

"…that there might be a happy ending? Such a thing does happen, my dear. Sometimes it takes a man to meet the right girl to realise he's with the wrong one."

Unfortunately what Matt had or hadn't realised was rather beside the point now. It was far too late for that.

"It was very foolish of me, really. I was on holiday after an unhappy break up, and I met him, and it all seemed like a bit of a dream, really." Except it had been real. It had been completely real for her, more vivid than anything else she had known, and she had thought he felt the same. "I think because of being on holiday, and the exoticness of it all, and the fact we had to be very discreet made it feel more intense than it was."

Evelyn Hillier poured her some more tea. "You know of course that I'm dying to ask you which one it was."

"I thought you might have guessed."

The two women looked at one another, and Cara saw that Evelyn had guessed. The sympathy in the older woman's eyes made her feel tearful herself.

"We saw the newspapers, of course, when we came back. Truthfully dear I don't think Peter realised a thing, but I did notice how you were more on edge at certain moments of the game. So I rather wondered then. And I did notice how he had his eyes on you at the after match party," Evelyn told her.

This gave Cara a pang. "I didn't realise you were there."

"We stayed just for one drink, early on. Rather more for a younger crowd those celebrations. But as I say I did wonder, and then when I saw the news about him I thought of you and I hoped that I might have been wrong. It's partly why I asked you to stay, not to assuage my own curiosity, but if I was right, I felt worried for you."

Cara sipped the hot drink. There was something wonderfully comforting about tea. And about being here, in this lovely home, with someone kind who understood.

"You must think it awful of me, I mean I knew he had a girlfriend. When I realised who he was, of course, I didn't actually realise the first times we spoke," Cara said.

"Not at all, my dear," Evelyn Hillier said. "It's not as though he was married. I might be scandalous in my view, but there's a considerable difference between having a ring on the finger or not. How quaint that you didn't even recognise him."

Matt may as well have twenty rings on his finger now, Cara thought. "I just feel very naive now. At least no one else there knew, or I hope they didn't. And what they printed in the papers afterwards, I had no idea about any of that. I felt so ashamed."

"You can't be blamed for what you didn't know," Evelyn told her. They sat in silence for a while, and then changed the subject to Evelyn's beautiful garden and how it would look in summer.

* * *

The subject of Matt wasn't explicitly raised by Evelyn Hillier again during Cara's stay, but she was very kind to her. They had persuaded her to stay with them until Monday morning so they could spend the whole of Sunday with her and she accepted.

Their world was very different to hers but Cara enjoyed herself greatly. It was a sanctuary for her. She hardly turned to her textbooks or the cricket-themed novels that Mr Hillier had offered her. Instead she lay on her bed and let her thoughts drift off. She was more tired than expected from the travel and perhaps the emotion of confiding in Evelyn.

The Hilliers took her for a drive on Sunday afternoon to see some local landmarks. "You must come and stay again when the weather is warmer, you're not seeing Knowlbury at its best," they told her. The village cricket pitch, Mr Hillier told her, was renowned in the area for being particularly scenic.

Before he drove Cara to the station on her final morning, Evelyn Hillier managed to have a few more words with her.

"Your situation has been very much on my mind," she said. "I do hope visiting us hasn't made the memories more painful. But have courage, my dear. And remember that while there is life there is always hope, even if sometimes a happy ending seems a very long way off."

Cara wasn't quite sure what she meant, but she assumed Evelyn was telling her that she would find love again. She thanked them for their hospitality and promised to visit again soon.

17. Stolen meeting

Matt told himself it was to get it out of his system. That it was the right thing to do. That he owed her, and himself. That it would help bring "closure", that clichéd term that he had always dismissed before.

But he had to see Cara one more time. The truth was that he simply wanted to. The urge to contact her and see her again was stronger than the rational arguments he made to himself against doing so.

He could have tried to ring her but he didn't think hearing her voice would be enough. So he drove to her town. He had asked for her address before she had left Sri Lanka, when he was still considering a very different outcome.

The journey took longer than he thought and he had left on a whim so it was late evening by the time he reached Cara's place. It took him back to his own student days: a quiet suburban street of small red-brick terraces, most of them shared houses or split into flats. Many had bicycles chained to the railings in front.

He found the right number and knocked on the door. For a moment as he waited there he thought of leaving again but then the door opened. A young woman stood there, about the same age as Cara.

"Can I help?" she asked.

Ann was used to odd friends of Fiona occasionally turning up at all hours so she wasn't overly disconcerted by a strange man appearing on the doorstep at night. That was student life for you, there was always someone trying to find a party or a study session somewhere. Besides which he also looked quite respectable even if he was older than most of their student friends. Fiona's friends tended to be more alternative but this man was clean cut, and very attractive.

Thinking all this as she saw him, Ann also realised that he looked strangely familiar. "Aren't you...?"

"Off Coronation Street? I get that a lot. No, I just look like him." Matt had used this strategy a few times, pretending to be the doppelganger of some soap star. People often thought they recognised him or even knew him, so he laid a false trail whenever he could.

Ann was frowning, even more confused. She'd be leafing through a television guide later on, trying to place whom he reminded her of.

"I'm actually a friend of Cara's cousin," he said. He hoped that Cara had a cousin, or that Ann would be unaware whether she did or not. "Is she in?"

"No, she's out for the evening. But you're welcome to wait here for her. She might not be back until late though."

Having come all this way, Matt couldn't wait that long.

"I'll go and meet her in the town. Do you know where she is?"

"Downtown. I mean it's a club," Ann said, seeing his confusion. "Called Downtown."

"Which is also down town? I'll find it." Matt thanked her and left.

* * *

Cara had been dragged out on the town by Fiona and some of her flamboyant friends yet again. Fiona was determined not to let her sit around and mope. "You're still looking tired and miserable all the time, it's much better to get out and distract yourself."

They had tried to persuade Ann to come but nightclubs weren't really her thing. She had a lot of study to do anyway.

Fiona was studying biochemistry like Cara, but most of her friends seemed to be doing theatre studies. They were a lively crowd and Cara was managing to enjoy herself.

She was slightly nervous that Declan might show up. He had been telephoning constantly, and if he thought she was out on the town he might come looking for her in the various pubs and bars frequented by the university students.

Just as she had managed to relax for a moment and forget her woes, while one of the theatre set was telling an outrageous anecdote, Fiona grabbed her arm.

"I think he's here," she said.

Cara froze and her heart sank. She really couldn't face another confrontation with Declan. He had shown up at her place while she had been away staying with the Hilliers and been so rude and demanding to Ann and Fiona about her whereabouts that they had threatened to call the police if he didn't leave.

"Where?" she asked Fiona, her eyes scanning the room nervously for someone who looked like Declan.

"There. The far end of the bar," Fiona said.

Cara looked and got an even bigger shock.

It was Matt.

* * *

Once he saw her, talking and laughing with some tall and glamorous young man, Matt felt a wrench in his guts that made him want to punch someone.

Knowing that Cara had every right to be talking and flirting with whomever she liked didn't help. Nor did knowing that it was wiser and better for her to have moved on. After all neither of them had made any promises and he had nothing to offer her.

But seeing her there, lovelier than he remembered, so young and vibrant and beautiful, was physically painful.

Because Matt knew in that moment what he had been trying to deny. That despite every intention to keep things casual he had let his feelings get involved. He had fallen for her.

That in itself was an understatement. Looking at her across the crowd, wearing a dress he wanted to tear off her even more than the blue slip she'd worn at the party, he wanted simply to be with her more than any other girl he had ever met.

And it was impossible.

Realising this, he also realised he couldn't disturb her peace again. It wouldn't be fair. It would only torment him even more and reopen any wounds she had. If she had wounds. It may have been completely casual for her, Matt thought. After all she hadn't tried to contact him.

He knew this was absurd. How in a million years could she have contacted him, with all those headlines? But he felt gutless that he hadn't at least tried to call her and explain. If he promised to call a girl he always had done, at least if it had gone as far and as long as things had with Cara.

It was no good, he would have to make this one, last, final glimpse of her his closure. The knowledge that she was well and happy and had moved on.

* * *

It was definitely him. Cara was so stunned she couldn't move. "What do you think he's doing here?" She tried to make it look as though she hadn't noticed, that she wasn't staring at him.

"Why do you think he's here?" Fiona asked. "He's hardly going to be coming to some dive like this for a night out, is he? He obviously came to see you."

Cara tried to think of why there might be another explanation that he was there. But there was nothing plausible. Why then, if he had come to see her, didn't he come over? She couldn't stand there and keep staring at him.

"Why don't you just go up to him, say hello?" Fiona asked.

Cara wanted to but she was paralysed. Maybe he wasn't coming over because he had seen her and changed his mind. She caught his eye and for a split second she thought he was going to approach her.

But then he put his drink down, turned, and left. She watched him climb the stairs to exit the club.

Exhilaration turned to devastation in an instant. Why had he gone? Was he coming back? How could she endure the rest of the night now?

"For god's sake, go after him," Fiona said. "He clearly bottled it."

It wasn't Fiona's urging that gave Cara the resolve to go. It was remembering Evelyn Hiller's words: "Have courage."

Whatever Matt wanted, whatever he had meant to say but had changed his mind about, she couldn't leave it like this. It was now or never.

* * *

Cara rushed up the stairs which wasn't easy as they were narrow and she had to push past people to get out.

She called out to him.

Matt stopped, turned. She came up to him.

They stood there for a while, gazing at one another. Feeling the hopelessness of it all.

"I didn't know," Matt said.

"You didn't know what?"

So many things. What being with her would lead to. What saying goodbye would feel like. What knowing he could never be with her again would be like. What seeing her again was like.

But there was something he had to clear up. "About the pregnancy. When I was with you, I didn't know."

Cara couldn't speak. She had suffered such terrible humiliation over the past weeks, feeling horribly betrayed, as though he had lied to her. Now reality was shifting yet again.

"If I had had any idea, I would never..." he broke off, still gazing at her. Yet deep down he was glad he hadn't known. She had been worth it even for those few snatched moments. Just to know what it should be like. Maybe, if he tried hard enough, he could get that feeling back again one day.

"What happened in Sri Lanka, I know what you said at the outset and I never had any expectations," Cara said. "But it wasn't just a senseless bit of fun for me. It ended up meaning something. I know you don't really know me that well and I just wanted you to know that."

She wasn't sure what she was saying but he took her into his arms and his lips came down on hers. He kissed her, tenderly, sweetly, both of them yearning for the other like a thirst.

His lips were warm and firm, just as she remembered. Familiar yet also those of a stranger. His touch on her was the same and it thrilled her: his hands in her hair, clasping around her back, encircling her. His height, the taste and smell of him, the shape of his muscles under her own hands. Matt. The one her whole heart and body longed for.

The last time, the last time, kept beating in Cara's head. Remember this forever.

All the clichés, all the stupid romance films she'd watched, love poems she would have laughed at before, everything made sense for a few moments. Time stood still. There were only the two of them in the world.

Yet even as he embraced her, as they clung together wanting never to break away, the world started creeping back in. The cold air of night, traffic passing by, the scent of the rain-wet pavement shining in the street light, the shouts of other revellers. The world swirled back around them and separated them once more.

Matt pulled back. "You know that I could stay here all night. But I have to get back."

"I know." She couldn't bear to say goodbye, to watch him walk away. So she went back into the club, into the darkness and the melee and the strobe lights that would hide her tears.

And Matt watched Cara go. Tried to make sense of why things happened as they did. Why they were supposed to happen "for a reason". What reason was this pain?

18. Persistent suitor

Fiona had urged her to "drown her sorrows" that night but Cara had barely drunk anything because she felt so numb and drawn out. When she woke in the morning she felt even worse, and was relieved that it was still the weekend. Fiona never seemed to get a hangover and was already flitting around the kitchen offering Cara a coffee, but Cara couldn't stomach anything.

She was hollow with misery. Last night had stirred everything up again. Knowing Matt hadn't lied to her or deliberately led her on just made it even worse somehow. She had nothing to blame him or hate him for.

"Want some toast?" Fiona asked, but even the thought of that turned Cara's stomach. "You've lost weight recently. Don't pine away to nothing."

Ann entered, back from her early church service. "Nice sermon?" Fiona asked.

Ann was never quite sure whether Fiona was mocking her about her church and her trainee vicar boyfriend, so she said "just the usual" and fetched herself a cup of tea. "By the way did your cousin manage to find you last night? Your cousin's friend, I mean," she asked Cara.

"Who?"

"The one who looks like that actor off Coronation Street, only I can't think which one," Ann said. "I said he could wait but he went to look for you in town."

Fiona and Cara exchanged a glance. That mystery was solved anyway.

"Yes, thank you, we saw him the club," Cara said.

"Who is it he looks like? I'm sure it will come to me. He was so familiar, really. I'm sure he must get annoyed with people mentioning it." Ann chattered on and Cara felt deeply uneasy. The last thing she wanted was Ann to actually recognise who Matt was. There would be absolutely no way to explain the situation. Not that she could think of right now, anyway.

The doorbell went and of course she immediately thought - hoped - it was Matt.

Fiona went to open it. Declan stood there, a huge bunch of roses in his hand. They were a very dark red colour that Cara had never cared for. It was probably a petty thing to notice, but she was reminded how little he had ever really listened to her or cared about her preferences and opinions.

Just as now. He still wouldn't give up despite her telling him again and again that it was over. Fiona had even offered to have one of her actor friends pose as Cara's new boyfriend but Cara had thought it wasn't necessary. Not yet, anyway.

She also didn't want to fan the flames. Hopefully Declan's persistence would eventually fizzle out, she didn't want him challenging some guy to a fight. Or a duel. She had a momentary image of Declan fighting Matt, with Matt shirtless and wielding a rapier like the cover of the lurid airport novel she still hadn't read, and smiled despite herself.

Unfortunately Declan interpreted her expression as an invitation. Nothing she could do could get rid of him from the doorstep, and in the end to her shock Fiona came out and tipped a jug of cold water on him. "Your flowers look a bit limp," she told him and slammed the door in his face.

He kept ringing the bell but they ignored it. On and on and on. They might have laughed over the water but the incessant ringing set everyone on edge.

"Honestly I really think you need to do something, it's getting beyond a joke," Fiona told her.

"Perhaps you should sit down and talk to him properly. Just one last time," Ann said.

Cara had already tried this. Multiple times.

"Then file a restraining order and have done with it," Fiona said. "He's never going to get the message otherwise."

This seemed needlessly drastic to Cara. Declan was just finding it hard to accept he no longer had control of her life. Hopefully he'd meet someone soon and move on.

When he had finally given up, or at least the ringing had stopped, Ann brought up Cara's "cousin's friend" again.

"He was very handsome, the man who called for you last night. Does he live nearby?"

Cara could see she was angling to find out if there were any romantic prospects there for Cara. Ann had been desperate to set her up with someone "to mend her heartbreak" since she had come back from Sri Lanka.

"No, in London somewhere. He had promised to look me up if he was in town. I expect he just felt obliged really." She was trying to shut the conversation down and it worked for the time being. Ann went off to her room because she was meeting her own boyfriend later for lunch, after he'd finished his duties at the second church service.

"Well, well," Fiona said when Ann had gone. "I wonder if she'll figure it out? You'd better keep the sports pages away from her."

Cara was more worried about Declan. "He will give up eventually, won't he? Maybe he'll get back with Lucinda?"

"I wouldn't bet on it. Let me know if you change your mind about getting a restraining order, I'd be happy to help you sort it out."

* * *

"Where were you last night?"

Matt had stood Chris up the previous evening. They were supposed to have been meeting in a local pub for a meal and a drink.

"Something came up," Matt told him. They were at training. It was a cold and bright spring morning, just the thing to clear his head.

Chris could read him like a book.

"Something or someone? Miggy?"

"No. Just other stuff." He apologised for not letting Chris know. "It was a bit last minute."

"Miggy rang, around seven. Couldn't get hold of your mobile apparently. I thought perhaps she'd managed to afterwards and that was where you were."

"No." Damn. He hadn't asked Chris to cover for him, of course, nor would he have. But now things probably looked really suspicious.

There were men that would compound a lie with other lies. When found out to be sneaking around, they would claim to have been planning a surprise, buying a gift or something. Matt wasn't one of them.

If Miggy asked him outright where he had been he would have to tell her something. It wasn't going to be the exact truth because given her current state it wouldn't be fair on her. But he wasn't going to try and pretend it was for her benefit either.

"I had to see an old friend," he said. If Chris accepted it then perhaps Miggy would too.

But Chris looked at him intently. "An old friend?" he asked. "A female friend?"

"It doesn't matter now, it's all dealt with," Matt said. He twirled his bat and prodded it on the grass, making a dent. It was a sign he was stressed.

Chris couldn't take the conversation any further because there were other players around. Specifically Jeremy Afford who fortunately had stopped stirring since they'd got back to England and Miggy's pregnancy had been revealed. He had some sense of decency, at least. Besides which he had no real proof that anything had happened. He was just piqued that his captain had cut in when he was trying to chat up a girl.

Afterwards Chris cornered Matt in the car park. "It's none of my business, but I don't think bottling it up is doing you any favours. Your play is off, I've never known you to mistime the ball so often. You're being short with some of the team, you face a PR disaster if it all goes to hell with Miggy."

Matt felt furious at Chris's words but knew it was true. And that he was only speaking out of friendship and concern. "It's all fine now. It's over," he told him.

"Tell me it's not that girl in Sri Lanka. Has she been calling? Making threats?"

"God no!" Matt was indignant at such an accusation being levelled at Cara. She was the sweetest girl, she was the last person on earth to try and harass him or blackmail him.

Chris could see from Matt's reaction that he'd struck a nerve. "It is her though, isn't it?" He knew Matt well enough to know that there hadn't been other exes or women on the side during the time he'd been with Miggy. The beautiful student in Sri Lanka was the first time he'd seen Matt's head turned for years.

"I just went to see her. I owed her an explanation."

Finally it was all making sense to Chris. No wonder Matt was in such a black mood. "You're only with Miggy because of the pregnancy, aren't you? You were going to dump her for that girl?" Before Matt could protest he continued. "You're clearly miserable about the situation and you're the world's worst actor. If I've noticed then Miggy will have too. Or she will. You're going to have to be honest with her. It will be better for both of you and the baby if you sort things out now."

The problem was that it wouldn't make any difference. Splitting up with Miggy wasn't going to fix the rest of his life. The thought of lawyers and custody battles and child support - he's seen enough blokes go through it - would just be an ongoing nightmare. Not something he could bring another person into, not now. Cara deserved better than that. She deserved better than him, someone who'd screwed up his life and relationships and was lying to everyone.

Right now Matt hated himself. He turned down Chris's offer of a beer. Nothing could make this better. He just had to hope that when the baby came it would change everything for the better. That he'd fall in love with it, and Miggy, and everything would be alright again.

19. A shock

Cara had food poisoning that morning from one of Fiona's infamous curries the night before.

"I'm sure it wasn't my cooking," Fiona said. "I'm fine and so's Ann. You must have a very sensitive stomach."

Ann agreed. "You were the only one to be ill after that takeaway last week."

"It's probably all the stress of everything," Fiona said. "With exams coming up," she added quickly, as Ann still had no idea what Cara was really stressed about.

Because Ann was still in the dark she started to fret about Cara's state of health. "You don't seem to be eating very well and you do seem quite strung out," she said. She kept nagging Cara until Cara finally agreed to see a doctor.

Fiona didn't disagree. "After being that sick you may need some antibiotics, if I really did give you E Coli," she said. She offered to accompany Cara as Ann had a tutorial that morning.

Cara managed to get an appointment for later that morning, and she and Fiona caught the bus to the surgery.

The doctor was a middle aged woman with an intelligent, matter-of-fact demeanour. She took Cara's blood pressure and pulse and temperature. "Nothing amiss there." Cara was starting to feel like a hypochondriac for even going.

"Normally there's no need to prescribe anything for food poisoning," the doctor told her. "Not unless you also have a urinary tract infection for example." She checked with Cara as to whether she had had any such symptoms, and Cara realised unfortunately that she did have.

"Not severe though," she said, hoping to avoid medication.

"We'd better give you a course nonetheless. Now, are you pregnant or currently trying to conceive?"

What a question. The irony of it in the circumstances. "No," Cara said.

The doctor consulted Cara's notes. She mentioned the contraceptive pill that Cara was currently taking. "You'll need to use other contraception until you've completed the antibiotics I'm going to prescribe you," she told her. "Also depending when you take your pill, the vomiting may have meant you didn't absorb it properly."

Cara didn't really want to admit that she had no real need of the pill now anyway. But something was niggling in her mind. "I know I should know this," she asked, "but if I had taken it a couple of hours late, might that have prevented it from working?"

"With what you're taking, an hour or so should be fine. Longer than that and you'll need to use other contraceptive measures for a week. Have you had a lapse?"

The flight to Sri Lanka. She'd been in such a rush that morning that she'd packed her pills without taking one, and hadn't been able to get to them until she landed. It hadn't been a big deal at the time of course, given that things had been over with Declan.

"I don't think so. I mean I'd know if I was pregnant, wouldn't I?"

The doctor looked at Cara above her reading glasses. "You might. Or you might not. I've known patients go for several months without realising. One even turned out to be having twins. When did you last have a menstrual period?"

Not since Sri Lanka. And not for some time before. Cara sat there, horrified, to only be realising this now. But she was sure things must be fine. After all, things had been very light since she'd started the pill.

"What sort of symptoms should I expect?"

The doctor reeled off a list and Cara's horror grew. Tiredness. Exhaustion. Nausea. Vomiting. Plus a few other things that she couldn't truly say she hadn't experienced.

"Given your uncertainty, it's best I don't prescribe these now. Why don't you go and take a test and have a look at your calendar, and come back this afternoon when we know where we are?" the doctor said.

Cara felt as though she were in a trance. The hollowness of her stomach from the illness and the tiredness didn't help. The doctor gave her some strict instructions about keeping hydrated, plus a leaflet about pregnancy and conception, and Cara went back to the waiting room. She didn't really know what to tell Fiona.

But Fiona spotted the leaflet. "What the hell's that?"

Cara couldn't discuss it right there. "Let's get out of here." She needed to sit down, to think about things. She was sure she was fine and was just having a panic due to her sleeplessness and being so sick earlier that morning.

The two of them found a café down the road and ordered drinks. Cara went for a fruit juice instead of a coffee, remembering the doctor's advice about fluid intake.

"Are you pregnant?"

"God no!" was Cara's first reaction. And then she looked worried. "I'm sure I'm not. I mean I'm almost sure. I'm on the pill, I've been on it for months."

"It's not a hundred per cent, you know," Fiona said.

"I know. And I might have got a bit messed up with taking it with the flights and the time zones," Cara said. "Anyway just to be on the safe side, the doctor wants me to take a test. I've never done that though, can you just buy them?"

Fiona started laughing. She apologised. "I'm sorry, this must be horribly stressful for you. It's just on top of everything, I can't imagine more of a total mess of a situation if you were." Her face was grave for a moment. "Please God tell me it's not Declan's though?"

There was no way it could be, fortunately. Or unfortunately. At least Declan was single and available. Cara shuddered at the thought of it being his. "Not without a virgin birth."

"That's more Ann's line. Goodness, she'll get a bit of a shock if you are."

Ann was the least of Cara's worries. Right now the priority was laying this nightmare to rest. For the doctor's peace of mind, she told herself. She knew within herself she was fine. She had to be.

* * *

"Is there a line?"

Fiona was outside the bathroom door. Cara was inside and the world was spinning around her. She clasped her arms around herself and closed her eyes and tried to make it all go away.

She ran the last few weeks back through her mind, as if rewinding a video tape. She wound it back to the Heathrow Airport and the departure lounge, and pressed pause. She would keep it there. Before she ever left for Sri Lanka. Before she met Matt. Then everything would be okay again.

"Cara? Are you alright?" Fiona was getting anxious. It had already been longer than the ten minutes required. She was worried Cara had fainted or something. Trying the handle she found it was unlocked, and pushed the door open.

Cara was sitting there, as white as a sheet.

The opened pregnancy test lay by the basin. Fiona glanced at it but had already guessed what she was going to see there.

It was unmistakeable. It was a strong, clear, bold line. Unequivocally a positive result. Not that "positive" seemed the right word in the circumstances.

There weren't really any words. There was only putting her arms around Cara, and telling her that everything would be alright. That she wasn't on her own. That the world wasn't ending.

They sat there for a while and then Fiona managed to get her to the sitting room, and went to make them a cup of tea. Only last week Cara had bought some decaffeinated teabags hoping they would help her sleep better. How ironic, and yet how useful now.

"Are you going to tell him?" Fiona asked.

It was the million dollar question. Not in a million years, was the answer.

"I can't do that to him. To her. He can't ever know about this," Cara said.

"He possibly has a right to know. Depending on what you do."

What would she do? Since she had found out, she could only imagine one path. "It's funny, I'm not religious like Ann is. I always thought if this happened to me that I'd just end it. But ever since I was at the doctor, when she first made me wonder about it, I could only imagine seeing it through."

"You mean having it? Keeping it?" Fiona asked.

"Yes. I know that's probably really foolish."

"It's not foolish at all, if it's what you want. You're an adult, by the time it arrives you'll have your degree. You should tell him though. You've got as much claim over him as she has now."

This was such an awful way to put it. Cara flinched. She found herself feeling sorry for Miggy, a woman she'd never even met.

She remembered the night when Matt had come to the club and told her that he hadn't known about the pregnancy. Although he hadn't said it explicitly, it was clear what he was implying. That he was staying with Miggy because of the baby, because he had to. Because he had no choice.

How could she trap him in the same way? She couldn't bear to be in Miggy's shoes, with a partner who was only there out of guilt. At least Miggy was hopefully blissfully ignorant about the reality of her circumstances. But Cara knew. She could never accept Matt being with her out of guilt or obligation. Resenting her, resenting the situation.

Not to mention the media fallout. The publicity over this could ruin his career. Fathering two children at the same time: the headlines would be appalling.

As Fiona had said, Cara had a choice. If it was her choice to keep it, then it was her choice to cope with it. Besides which she was the one who had made the mistake with her contraception. If she had realised, perhaps she could have taken emergency measures at the time.

She tried explaining this. Fiona rolled her eyes. "I wouldn't be nearly so noble in your shoes. Life isn't a fairy-tale."

That was something Cara could certainly agree with. Never had a happy ending seemed more remote.

20. Calculations

The test series against Pakistan had been a welcome distraction that month for Matt. Just being able to get away to Manchester for a week felt like an escape. Back to his old life.

England had drawn the series which was disappointing, but Matt had bigger things on his mind.

"You must be disappointed, missing out on a fifth consecutive win," a reporter asked him in the post-test press conference.

Matt gave a polite but neutral answer.

"Would you say England is losing momentum? Not showing the same spirit at Lord's, or in Karachi last November?" another cricket writer asked him.

Matt hated questions like these. The journalist had already decided what tone to take with his story, and whatever Matt said would be twisted into a negative statement. He gave a formulaic response.

There were a couple of questions about the upcoming Ashes series against Australia that summer and the conference was wound up.

Matt escaped to the bar to join the rest of his teammates where the conversation turned to Australia once again. The Ashes, a five-match series that England played against Australia every couple of years, were cricket's most celebrated rivalry.

"You taking any time off for the arrival?" someone asked Matt. "When's it due?"

"Not until August." Between the third and fourth tests from what the doctors had said. Matt still hadn't decided what to do.

He noticed Chris frown but didn't think much of it.

Talk turned to other topics and Matt found himself drinking more beer than he should. He was drinking too much these days generally and he needed to put a lid on it. He resolved to do so when he was back home in London. A fresh start. After all he wanted to be at peak fitness for the Ashes series. England hadn't won a series against Australia for over a decade and the pressure was really mounting.

Chris urged him to stay for another round when a group of them got up to go. Matt tried to decline. "I've already had several too many. We've got this dinner later."

"I know. Just have a coke."

Matt ordered a soft drink and sat down by Chris. "Something on your mind."

"Not on mine, possibly there should be on yours. What date's this kid arriving?"

"The doctors say the twenty-first of August, but it may not arrive exactly on that day." Matt had been doing his homework. Or rather Miggy had been giving him lectures.

"You absolutely sure about that?"

Now it was Matt's turn to look puzzled. "They seem to be fairly confident about the dates, I don't know how they work it out."

Chris drained his own pint. "You may have done Engineering, not Maths or Biology, but it might be time to get out your calculator. And have a look at your calendar last year. Nine months, remember."

"What are you on about?"

Chris suddenly looked weary. Concerned, and weary. Matt felt guilty because he knew Chris had his own issues but all the support in their friendship had been one way recently.

"It really isn't my business and I'm not a medic. Just consider checking all the dates."

* * *

Matt wasn't entirely sure what Chris was getting at. He thought that Chris must be saying the doctors were mistaken, perhaps that it would fall right at the start of the Ashes series which would be a bit more of a hassle in terms of taking time off.

He worked out the months in his head as he sat in the back of a taxi. Nine months back from mid-August was mid-November last year. Which was the previous England tour to Pakistan.

It was taking a while for the light to dawn, partly because of the enormity of what Chris was possibly suggesting.

The taxi driver was Asian. "Have you got kids?" Matt asked him.

"Four. Two at university, and my youngest son is also a very keen cricketer." Matt got the usual spiel and promised to autograph something for the boy.

It was all turning over in Matt's head. Dates and calendar months and Pakistan.

His sister had a flatmate who was a nurse. Once he had paid the cab driver and was by himself again, Matt rang them. "Can you put Jenni on?"

"What for? Is something wrong with Miggy?" His sister wasn't any keener on Miggy than his parents were, but she was looking forward to aunthood.

Matt didn't really know how to phrase what he wanted to ask. The fact that he was asking at all was potentially compromising.

"I wanted some info about pregnancy dates. It's for a present," he said. He was sick of lying but if Chris's comments were a wild goose chase it was better not to stir things up.

Jenni came on the other end of the line. She came from Dublin and he had always liked her accent. "Can I help?"

"It's just about pregnancy dates. For an anniversary present."

"You're a romantic. Most blokes I know are clueless about it all. What did you want to know?" Jenni asked.

Matt had been happily clueless before but the time for that was past. "How accurate is the due date the doctors give you? And can you work out, you know, when you must have..." He stumbled, embarrassed.

"The conception?" He could hear the amusement in her tone. "The due dates are pretty accurate, they base it on the last cycle. Naegele's rule, subtract three months and add a week. So if you want to figure out when you conceived it, just do the reverse, and add a week or so."

September, October, November. Mid-November. "Thanks."

Exactly nine months ago Matt had been in Pakistan and Miggy had been in Peru. Or she might have been back in England by then, he couldn't remember, but she had never come on the tour. She'd left for Peru half way through October. He hadn't seen her again until mid-December, it had been their longest time apart.

Matt was too distracted to want to go to the cricket dinner that evening but as captain, duty came first. What he wanted to do was get a biology textbook and try to get his facts straight. And then, if it didn't manage to explain the discrepancies that Chris and now Jenni had drawn his attention to, he had to figure out some way to broach the subject with Miggy.

* * *

The next day was a Tuesday and Matt found a bookshop first thing and bought three separate books on pregnancy. He noticed the shop assistant smirking, she had probably recognised him, but he didn't care. If she wanted to leak a story to the papers about "England captain swots up on fatherhood" she was welcome to. It made no difference to him.

He found a nearby café that wasn't too busy and ordered a double espresso. It grew cold on the table as he studied his new books.

Each one told him the same thing.

There was no way the baby could have been conceived before November or after mid-December unless the doctors were completely wrong in their dating of the pregnancy.

Knowing more than he had ever wanted to know about fertility timing and early foetal development, Matt headed back to London working out reasons in his mind why the doctors must be wrong. Miggy was always watching her weight. Maybe that affected

126

the size? Maybe it was growth restricted, there had been a horrible and worrying paragraph about that in one of the books.

"Another coffee?" No thanks, he hadn't even drunk the first one. Matt needed harder stuff than caffeine, not that he was going to indulge in anything. He was resolute about that. Once he decided something he stuck to it and that was part of the problem now.

The books were supposed to have allayed his concern. To give him an answer, not further confusion. Or perhaps they were giving him an answer but it wasn't the one he wanted. He was still sure that a medical error or anomaly could explain things.

He even hoped it could, though the reverse could mean an entirely different situation was about to unfold.

But the complications of it all, the overwhelming drama and humiliation and emotion: right now he wasn't sure if he could face that. He couldn't even start to think how it would play out in the press. How could you hide something like this, given how public Miggy had been? He'd also reached a sort of peace, so he thought, with the situation. He had become accustomed to it.

Maybe ignorance was bliss?

Matt cursed Chris in his mind. It felt like extra stress, extra pressure, at a time when he needed it least.

As he walked to his flat he saw a woman across the road who for a fleeting moment reminded him of Cara. It was enough to bring it all flooding back.

He still wasn't over it. Because of her, he needed to know.

Whatever was going on, he had to know. For all their sakes.

21. Revelations

Cara had been worried about Ann's reaction to her news but Ann was just as supportive as Fiona was. She felt very lucky to have them both as her friends.

They were sitting under a tree on the lawns in front of some of the university buildings. It was lovely and shady in the late spring sun. People milled about and spread books and study notes out over the lawn. There was a growing sense of camaraderie among all the final year students who were taking exams soon.

Ann of course first assumed that the baby was Declan's and it was doubly awkward trying to explain the real situation.

"I'm sorry I didn't tell you, it was all over and I felt so ashamed about it," Cara said.

"I wouldn't have judged you. I just feel bad that you've been going through all this alone." Ann was silent for a moment. "That was him, wasn't it, who came round here that night? I can't believe I thought he was some soap star. He's in the papers all the time. Does he know about the baby?"

Cara explained the same that she had said to Fiona, that there was no way she could ever tell him. "I can't wreck his life, and her life. Not now, anyway."

Ann was still thinking about the night Matt had visited their home. "Why did he come round then, if he didn't know?"

"I think he felt bad for never contacting me." It was partly true. Anything else needed to be forgotten. It was one moment, a lapse on his part, a lapse on hers to have worn her heart on her sleeve like that.

She still remembered the kiss though. She would remember it until her dying day.

"People are going to ask about the father. What will you tell them?" Ann asked.

Cara had already thought of this. "I'll tell them it was a one night stand in Sri Lanka and he didn't want to be involved." She didn't care if it made her sound cheap. The alternative - the truth - was impossible to contemplate.

"Were you really in love with him?"

"Yes, I think so." Cara said it partly because she knew it would make Ann feel easier about the situation if it hadn't been just lust. And partly because it was true. She should be over him by now, perhaps, but she wasn't. Having his baby only made her feelings even stronger.

She would learn to bury these emotions in time. Perhaps one day she would even meet someone else although she couldn't imagine that in a million years right now.

"You'll have to tell your child, one day. For now you have to figure out what you're going to do after graduation."

This one was easy. She would simply look for a job as she had always planned to. After all, she wasn't due until November. It seemed forever away.

"How have your family taken it?" Ann asked.

They didn't know yet. "I wanted to tell them in person. I'm going to go down next week and break the news."

They would be shocked, of course, but hopefully there wouldn't be a catastrophic scene. Cara's parents were fairly stoical people and should take it in her stride. One of her cousins had had an accidental pregnancy a couple of years ago, to a man who turned out to be married, and everyone had rallied round.

* * *

Sure enough her parents took the news on the chin. Her mother was the kind of person who always looked for silver linings. "At least it means that awful Declan is permanently out of the picture."

"Why did no one tell me he was so awful? Since we split up everyone has been telling me how much they disliked him," Cara said.

"You were besotted. You can't tell someone anything when they're like that," her mother said.

Her older brother Will chimed in. "Seriously Cara he was such a creep. We were planning some kind of intervention before the wedding. Thank God he's out of the way now."

Declan wasn't quite out of the way. He was still being a bit of a pest, he had turned up to one of her lectures the other day and tried to make a scene. Fiona had had to get the university staff to escort him forcibly off the premises.

He didn't know about the pregnancy yet of course. Once she told him he should finally get the message, it just hadn't been a priority to sort out yet.

It was nice being home. Safe and familiar and conventional. Her father doing something in his vegetable garden and her mother rolling pastry for a pie. She finished and washed her hands of flour, drying them on her apron as she sat down at the kitchen table with her two children.

"I do think this man should be stepping up to his responsibilities," her mother told her.

"Unless he's as bad as Declan in which case don't bother. I'll be the world's greatest uncle instead."

Cara wanted to hug her brother. He worked in the north of England and she had missed him greatly since he left home. She was glad he had come back for a visit the same weekend as her.

"It's just difficult. I think… he was married," Cara improvised. Another fib. But it was kind of true.

"Married? Goodness gracious, what were you thinking?"

"I wasn't thinking, was I? I was all mixed up over Declan." The real truth was that from the moment Matt had first kissed her, Declan might as well never have existed. She had barely given him a thought from that time onwards.

"He might be a murderer or something," Will said. He had a copy of the Telegraph and was reading the sports pages. Cara suffered fresh agony seeing a photo of Matt on the back page. "Fatherhood won't disrupt Ashes focus". She had intended to avoid reading or hearing anything about him, deciding it was for the best, but his name seemed to be everywhere. She also knew she would eventually give in and read every word once her family were out of the room.

Cara thought of the Hilliers who were devoted readers of the Telegraph. Evelyn Hiller would doubtless read that very same article. She wondered what Evelyn's reaction would be to her latest news. Horrified, probably.

* * *

After their parents had gone to bed, Cara and Will sat up watching television. Cara remembered all the years when as children they had been sent to bed first. Now with what had happened her childhood was really behind her. She was about to become the older generation.

There was an old Bond film on but they'd both seen it before, many times.

"There's something you're not telling us, isn't there?" Will said. "Is it actually Declan's but you don't want it to be?"

Cara struggled to find a way to explain the embarrassing truth. "There's no way it could be. Declan had rather traditional ideas about things."

Will laughed. "What a weirdo. So whose is it really then?"

She repeated the story of the probably-married near-stranger in Sri Lanka.

"I know that's not you, Cara," Will said. "It was obviously someone you liked, wasn't it?"

"Yes, it was."

"Does he actually know about the pregnancy?"

"No, I can't tell him. There are reasons."

"What reasons?" her brother asked. "It might change everything for the better if you did tell him. If I got a girl pregnant

I'd want to know. Even if I hadn't planned to settle down I might think of making a go of it."

"That's just it. I wouldn't want him under those circumstances. It would feel like I'd pressured him into it," Cara said.

"But you're not even giving him a chance."

"It's just there are really difficult circumstances. He was already involved with someone, and she's..." She broke off, feeling too ashamed to even say the words.

"Don't tell me this bastard has knocked two women up at once?"

Cara felt her face grow red. Her brother had always been too perceptive for his own good. Or rather for the good of anyone around him who was trying to conceal something. Despite herself her eyes flicked to the photo of Matt on the back page of the paper, which was now on the side table next to her brother.

Will saw her glance at it. "Babies are everywhere, aren't they? Did I tell you Jason and Anna are having a kid? Not planned either but they're making the best of it." Jason was an old school friend of his. "At least your mystery man isn't someone like that," he said, indicating the photo of Matt. "Now that would be bloody awkward, all over the newspapers."

He meant it as a joke but Cara felt so mortified she could hardly breathe or speak. She should have quickly laughed it off but she was paralysed.

Will saw the strange expression on her face. He was silent, looking at her, thinking hard. "You were in Sri Lanka in February, weren't you? Was that when England were playing? There's no way..."

He picked up the paper and looked at the photo and back at Cara.

"It's not, is it? Come on, Cara, talk to me. Don't wind me up."

She couldn't wind anything up. What she could do was cry, which is what she did. She had been bottling it up since the pregnancy test, forcing herself to stay calm. To plan, to try and be practical.

The reality was that she felt absolutely alone. Even though her flatmates knew she still felt like she was carrying this terrible burden that no one else could know about.

Will swore under his breath. "Come here." He put his arms around her, exactly the big brother support she needed right now. "It's OK, I won't tell Mum and Dad. Not if you don't want them to know." Cara hugged him, still unable to speak.

"I should have guessed earlier it would be something like this, for you to be so secretive about it," he said. "But we're all here for you."

22. Confrontation

It was the hardest conversation Matt had ever had to have. It was going to be awful if he was right and awful if he was wrong. But something of this magnitude couldn't be buried. It would hang over him every day, taint his future happiness with his child - if it was his child - if he didn't know.

A lot of men in his situation might have felt angry. But Matt didn't, essentially because he knew he didn't love Miggy. If it was his baby he would stand by her and he would try to love her in time. If it wasn't his then being free again would outweigh any hurt pride. Sure - things would be excruciating for a while publicity-wise, you couldn't hush up something like this up - but he'd get through it.

At the end of the day he did care for Miggy. His lack of love for her made him care for her more, in a way. He didn't want her to be hurt. He had felt guilty because he loved someone else and couldn't stop thinking about her. But perhaps, if there was a chance it wasn't his, it meant that Miggy didn't care for him as much as he had thought either.

There was the issue of why she had lied to him, if she had lied. Or maybe she was genuinely mistaken. She could be surprisingly ditzy about certain things as much as she was astute about others.

The only thing that mattered was the truth, and getting it gently, and fixing things between them if he'd got it all wrong.

Matt just hoped that raising his doubts wouldn't fracture their relationship irrevocably. They had had some good times after all. Maybe they would again in future.

Miggy was at her place, curled up on the couch reading a pregnancy book. Ironically it was one of the same ones he'd bought in Manchester. They still more or less alternated between his place and hers, they'd had vague conversations about finding a new place with an extra bedroom but it hadn't gone anywhere.

He sat down on a chair opposite her. "I need to ask you something. If I've got it all wrong you can call me an idiot and put it down to male panic over fatherhood or whatever." She was looking directly at him now. Her face was unreadable.

"Is there a chance this baby isn't mine?"

It was out there. The words hung in the air and he couldn't take them back now.

She closed the book. She suddenly looked a lot more tired, as though the serenity and confidence she had been exuding these past weeks were a masque, now dissolved.

"I'm not sure. There's a chance, yes."

"It was the dates. There were nearly two months that we weren't together." He knew he didn't need to explain it.

Now she was explaining herself. "When I found out I honestly didn't know. I just assumed it was yours, I mean we've been together for ages. It was only after a while that I wondered."

"All the headlines, the interviews when I got back? Why the hell did you do that if you weren't sure?" Matt hadn't meant to raise his voice but remembering what he had gone through at the airport and afterwards, he felt frustrated.

Miggy looked contrite. "I suppose it was my way of telling myself that it had to be yours. That it was best if it was yours. It made it a done deal."

He still hadn't asked whose it was but that felt strangely unimportant.

"Did you want it to be mine?"

She didn't speak for a long time. "Honestly? I don't think so. I don't think I wanted it to be anyone's. It just happened, and by the time I found out it was so far advanced that it just wasn't easy to make decisions I might otherwise have made. So I thought I should make the best of it. That we should make the best of it.

Otherwise it would just be so difficult for both of us. Even though if it hadn't happened…"

She didn't finish the sentence. He could guess what she was going to say. That her heart wasn't really in the relationship any more than his was.

"So there's someone else?" He couldn't feel anger or jealousy, not that he had any right to. He actually found himself feeling sorry for Miggy. The house of cards was tumbling down and she had more to lose than he did.

"Briefly. In Peru. You know how it is, everyone's away from home, too many drinks. Not that that's any excuse but you must see the same thing on tour." Matt winced at the truth of this. "He was a photographer. The dates do match rather perfectly. I should have told you earlier and I'm very sorry I didn't."

"Is there any chance it's mine?" he asked.

"I don't think so. I truly did think so, but with every scan it seemed to get less and less likely that the doctors could have made a mistake. I had no idea until this all started how accurate they could be with the dates."

It was Matt's turn to confess. "You weren't the only one who had too many drinks. Only in Sri Lanka though, not before."

He could see the mixed emotions in her eyes. "Maybe the fact that we both did, at the same time, is telling us something."

That it was over. That it would be over, if it wasn't for the pregnancy.

"So where do we go from here?" Thinking about what lay ahead, given their public status, seemed so overwhelming that he partly understood why she had taken the route she had. Less humiliating for both of them just to pretend that it was his and everything was okay.

"I don't know. I keep hoping that JJ will come up with something miraculous." JJ was her publicist. "Go underground for a while. Brazen it out. Pull a rabbit out of a hat. I honestly don't know. It's all getting so close."

She rested her hand on her stomach. "It's all surreal. I really have wanted to tell you for a while. I was planning to when I wanted to go for a weekend in the country last month, only our schedules didn't mesh."

As usual. It had been a problem throughout their relationship.

"Everything just snowballed," Miggy continued. "I know lying was awful. But I didn't know for sure and I still don't. I'll do a test, of course. Though it may be rather obvious."

"Obvious?"

"The photographer was Peruvian." She started laughing. "What a bloody mess. And you didn't deserve any of this."

Matt knew then that Miggy was planning to brazen this out. She would celebrate it as an "oops", it would be part of her eccentric, aristocratic IT-girl persona. He cringed to think of the interviews she would likely give.

"If it does turn out to be mine? I'm not going to leave you in the lurch," he said.

"Then we'll co-parent, as friends. I don't think either of us is really ready to settle down, do you? Or maybe you are, but I'm not. I can't think of anyone who would be a better father than you. So I wish it was yours, but I fear that it's almost certainly not."

* * *

The funny thing was that Matt still felt a sense of loss. Even though he hadn't wanted the baby, or at least a baby with Miggy, he'd tried so hard to feel positive about the idea that it had partly worked.

He felt a strange disappointment now. The baby had started to take form in his mind, he had had ideas about it and now it wasn't to be. But he also felt a huge amount of relief. Not specifically that it wasn't his but that he and Miggy were no longer yoked together by something.

He was also feeling expectation at the thought of seeing Cara again.

Would she still want him? He had put her through hell with what had happened. He remembered how she had walked away from him that night without even saying goodbye. She had confessed her true feelings to him and he hadn't been able to say anything back. To have been honest.

It felt wrong to go straight from Miggy to Cara. He was torn between giving it some time for decency's sake - the press knew nothing yet, of course - and wasting no more time. He remembered the young men around Cara in the nightclub. She wouldn't be available forever.

It might even be too late now.

He had rung Chris but got his voicemail and left a single message. "Pakistan - you were right."

When Chris finally called him back he was full of sympathy. "Just hold your head up and damn them all. And don't go rushing into something else too quickly. Dragging another person into this will only complicate it." He meant Cara. He knew Matt could be impulsive, he's certainly been impulsive enough in Sri Lanka.

Protecting Cara was now Matt's main concern. The newspapers were going to make an absolute meal of this, JJ had already warned Miggy that there was a limit to how far even he could stage manage it. "And I've spun murders into a feel-good feature."

Matt longed to escape somewhere and batten down the hatches until the worst of the media storm had passed. But with excitement ramping up over the upcoming Ashes series he was forced to face journalists and be frequently quoted in the press.

At some point it would all come out. Should he wait and let Cara find out that way? Or should he ignore Chris and his advice, and go and see her immediately?

Against his own wiser instinct to be patient, at the first opportunity Matt found himself driving to see Cara. He simply couldn't wait any longer. He needed her.

23. Interference

Despite everyone telling her the morning sickness would get better in the second trimester, Cara actually felt worse. She'd had to miss lectures that morning because she felt so queasy. She had a routine doctor's appointment in the afternoon so decided to rest at home until then.

Ann and Fiona were reluctant to leave her but she assured them she would be alright. "I'm not actually ill. Once this passes I'll be fine."

So she stayed at home, sipping herbal tea and hoping that the horrible feeling of nausea and dizziness would subside. Because she was at a low ebb, when the doorbell went she opened it without thinking to put the chain across first.

"Hello Cara."

It was Declan. He stepped inside the door before she could try and tell him to go away. She was too weak to force him to leave so she let him come in. Maybe it was time for that final conversation.

"Are you ill?" He saw that she was wearing a dressing gown at a time when she was normally up and about.

"Not exactly. Just not one hundred per cent."

"If you'll only come back with me I could look after you," he said. "You shouldn't be alone like this."

She was going to have to tell him or he would never give up. She plucked up her courage.

"Declan, it's over between us, absolutely. Things have changed for me. Even if I wanted to get back with you, and I don't, there are other things going on now."

"Is there someone else?"

Cara was startled by the hostility and fury in his eyes as he asked this.

"No. Not any more. But there was, and I'm pregnant."

"You bloody whore." He suddenly slapped her across the face. Stunned, she pressed her hand to her cheek, terrified. He had never been like this before, never shown any predisposition to violence.

Declan dropped down to sit on a chair and put his head in his hands.

He was talking and muttering to himself now, starting to rant. "All the same. Nothing but bitches betraying you, sleeping with every man in sight. Just can't keep their legs shut. But maybe it's a sign. Maybe I'm meant to save her."

Cara realised there was something seriously wrong with him. She was very frightened.

He looked up at her and it was as though he was another person. He smiled at her but it was like a mask. "It's OK, we can do this together. You and me and the baby. I'll take care of everything. You don't have to worry about anything any more. It is my baby but you've just forgotten."

The fear and the nausea were overcoming her. "I have to go to the bathroom." She dashed there and closed the door. She wished desperately that she could lock the door, there had been a key but someone had lost it. With just being three girls it hadn't been a priority to call a locksmith, you could just hang an "occupied" sign on the door if you needed to.

She vomited, feeling weak and shaky. She was fearful Declan would try to come in but he didn't. She sat on the floor, leaning against the bathtub. She was so tired. Maybe if she just put her head down on a towel for a moment the room would stop spinning.

Feeling safer inside the bathroom, despite the lack of lock, she curled up on the floor and lay there, exhausted, not wanting to move. Hoping that Declan would go, or that Fiona or Ann would come back. Wishing desperately that she was anywhere else except stuck, sick, in a house with a clearly disturbed and possibly dangerous ex-boyfriend.

* * *

Matt had no idea if Cara would be home or at university, but since he knew her address it seemed easiest to try that first.

He also had no idea how she would react to it all. His whole life was in turmoil but he felt that she would be the one person who would understand. It was selfish, no doubt, to drag her into it all but if she felt even a fraction of what he thought he felt for her, she would want him to. So he hoped.

He knocked on the door and it was answered by a thin, nondescript man. "Is Cara in?" Matt asked.

"Who's asking?" The man had a rather sneery look. Matt disliked him on sight, but then he found himself disliking any man that seemed close to Cara. He was really going to have to get his possessiveness in check. It would be okay once he was finally with her, officially. It was not being able to let people know that he was with her that had driven him so mad in Sri Lanka.

"I'm Matt."

"Of course you are." The thin man lifted his eyebrows in amused recognition but did not budge from the doorway.

"Is Cara there? I need to see her urgently."

"She's indisposed. I'm Declan, by the way." He said it in a way that assumed that Matt would know who he was, which of course he did.

This smug worm was Cara's ex-fiancé? What the hell was he doing here?

"Is she alright? Is something wrong?" Matt asked.

Declan smiled and it wasn't a pleasant smile. A smirk might be the best way to describe it. Matt had to grit his teeth not to try and push past him. He was losing his patience.

"She's quite alright, thanks," Declan told him.

He wasn't budging. Matt glared at him. The two of them were deadlocked. Matt knew who Declan was and what his connection to Cara was. Declan had recognised who Matt was and half guessed his connection to Cara. If he had been in any doubt then Matt's obvious fury at Declan blocking him pretty much gave it away.

Matt tried one more time. "If you could just let her know I'm here. I would really like to see her."

"That's not possible right now. I'll let her know you called." Matt knew that Declan would do no such thing, and Declan knew that Matt knew.

"Is she ill?"

Declan played his trump card. "It's nothing that isn't to be expected. Just morning sickness, we're having a baby."

What?

It sent Matt reeling.

He was utterly floored.

How was this possible?

He knew how, of course, but why? What the hell was Cara thinking of? How could she jump straight back into bed with this shocking creep and let herself get knocked up by him?

The irony of her being pregnant to someone else was not lost on him. Clearly Cara had firmly intended to move on, and had done so.

There wasn't really a lot left to say. If Matt had thought that seeing her being chatted up by other guys in the nightclub was a punch in the guts, this absolutely blew him away.

He managed to mutter something like "give her my congratulations" and then he left in a blur. He felt far more of a fool now than from any of Miggy's deception.

Better to know now than later. And better not to have seen her, he thought, as it might have been more than he could take.

* * *

Declan closed the door, satisfied that they had seen the last of Matt. Cara clearly needed protecting from herself.

He went outside the bathroom and knocked. "Are you alright in there?"

142

Cara was still feeling terrible and it was getting near to her doctor's appointment. "I'm fine. Just give me a moment."

She splashed her face with water and steeled herself to face him. Hopefully the appointment would be a good excuse for him to leave.

She tried to fake a smile when she came back into the living room. "It's all OK now. Was there someone at the door before?"

"Just someone with the wrong number. He wanted next door."

Cara had no reason not to believe him but she had had the strong feeling while in the bathroom that there had been a caller for her. She didn't know why, she wasn't expecting a parcel or anything. It was probably wishful thinking that it was someone to help her get rid of Declan.

She tried to pretend that none of the weirdness had happened before. She put his hitting her down to shock, something completely out of character. A one-off.

"Thank you for coming round, perhaps we can go for coffee some time." Maybe if she kidded him that the lines of communication were open he would give up and go away. Then she should do as Fiona had been urging her to do for ages and file for a restraining order. "For now though I have to get to the hospital, I've got an appointment."

"You didn't mention it before," Declan said. His tone was accusatory. He thought she was lying.

"It's on the calendar."

He went to look, and satisfied that she was telling him the truth, he said he would drive her there. "You'll be late otherwise."

It was the last thing Cara wanted, to spend even ten minutes more with him.

"Thanks but it's a quick bus ride," she said.

"I don't think so. Not in your condition."

She was starting to feel panicked again, wondering if she could ever get away from him. She was also exhausted and sick and she wanted to see her doctor. At least if he drove her there she could get rid of him once she was inside. She could perhaps ask the doctor to get the receptionist to call Fiona or Ann to pick her up.

"If you really don't mind, that would be very kind." If she treated him normally perhaps he would calm down and become normal again. He had seriously frightened her before with his mutterings, and the controlling way he kept speaking to her. She wondered if he was having some kind of a breakdown.

Feeling a deep sense of unease she got her bag and followed Declan into his car.

Five minutes later he had driven straight past the doctor's surgery, out of town and out onto the motorway despite her protestations, and she realised she had made the worst decision of her life.

24. Kidnapped

Fiona didn't consider herself much of a psychic but she'd had a funny feeling leaving Cara alone that morning. She couldn't put her finger on why, but her unease was enough to make her turn down a coffee with a classmate after lectures and head straight home instead.

The flat was silent when she got there. She remembered Cara had had an appointment earlier in the afternoon, but she should have been back by now. Maybe she had gone to the supermarket?

The answerphone light was flashing so she pressed it while putting the kettle on and sorting out some post that had arrived. It was the doctor's surgery.

"We were sorry not to see you at your appointment today. Please give me a call to reschedule and we'll try to fit you in before the end of the week."

Odd. So Cara had missed her medical appointment. She had been quite conscientious about her health since finding out she was pregnant so Fiona was surprised she had missed it without even calling to cancel.

She checked Cara's bedroom in case she was asleep but it was empty. Cara's bag was gone as well as the folder in which she kept her pregnancy information. Fiona remembered seeing it on the coffee table that morning.

Puzzled but not yet overly worried she drank her cup of tea and read a couple of letters, before hearing the door go. "Cara, is that you?"

It was Ann arriving back from classes. "No, isn't she here?"

"She must be out shopping."

Fiona didn't mention the missed appointment. It was still light outside and maybe Cara had bumped into someone in town.

They watched some television, supper came and went, and now it was dark and there was still no sign of Cara. The clock ticked on. Both girls were feeling uneasy now. It was an awkward situation because they usually kept one another informed about their whereabouts, but not always. They were all adults and independent. No one was specifically watching over anyone else.

It was Fiona who finally broke the silence.

"I'm a bit worried about her. She didn't go to the doctor's today, and I don't remember her saying she had anything else to do."

"Me neither. And she's been so sick and tired I would expect her to have come home and gone to bed by now."

They tried ringing round Cara's friends but no one they got through to had heard anything from her, nor had expected to. Ann even tried Declan but his number rang out. They thought it was unlikely that Cara had gone home, given she'd only been at her parents' place the previous weekend. "I don't want to worry her family unnecessarily," Fiona said.

"We should at least rule it out." So they rang, but there was no answer.

They both sat up late that night, watching TV and trying to pretend they weren't as worried as they were. Eventually it got to midnight and Fiona said they needed to make a decision. "We can leave it until morning, or we can put out a call now. I'd sleep better knowing we'd at least tried something. Better to wake up and feel silly when she strolls in for breakfast than having done nothing."

"Let's ring the hospital then. At least that will rule out if she has been in an accident or fallen unwell. No news is probably good news," Ann said.

The hospital had no record of anyone by Cara's name being admitted in the last 24 hours, which was a relief but didn't help their unease.

"I'll try the police. They probably won't do anything until morning anyway, but it can't hurt. After all she is pregnant."

Fiona ended up having to give a lot of answers as to Cara's mental state, and was told to call again in the morning if Cara showed up.

* * *

Cara was furious and terrified. Mainly she was desperately worried for the baby in case Declan did something stupid. He had sped along the motorway at breakneck speed: she found herself alternately fearful that he would lose control and kill them both, and hopeful that if he kept up the pace the police would flag him down for speeding.

But there were no patrol cars on the road. Declan exited the motorway onto some country roads that she didn't recognise. Past a village. Past a farm. She was trying to remember the route so she could get back to the nearest building if she managed to get away from him.

Eventually he turned off a deserted stretch of road down another road that was more of a track. At the end there was a small cottage. Cara noticed the garden was quite overgrown.

"Where are we?" she asked, trying to keep her voice light. She didn't dare scream at him for fear of antagonising him. He had already hit her once and was clearly not normal. Or what she had thought was his normal self, anyway.

"You'll like it. It will be a nice home for us," he said. "You'll be safe here. No one to disturb you."

"Is it your cottage?" Cara asked.

"It belongs to my aunt, but she lives most of the year in South Africa."

Perhaps if she put on a pretence of being happy with the situation, of letting him think she was going along with his plans, he might relax enough not to be dangerous. Or even to let her escape.

"You never mentioned you had an aunt in South Africa," she said.

"There's a lot you don't know about me, Cara. If you did you wouldn't be doing the things you did… but we won't talk about that now. We have all the time in the world to get to know one another properly again."

If she hadn't known him properly during their relationship, and she could well believe that now, it was because he had held her at arm's length. He had worn a mask while behind it he acted like a completely different person. Maybe that was why she had fallen for him so badly before, to the point of agreeing to marry him. Because she wrongly thought he had "hidden depths" or mistook his furtiveness for reserve.

Declan opened the door with a key. Inside the cottage seemed clean but a bit musty. "Your aunt won't mind, will she?" Cara asked. "When is she due back?" Please let it be very soon, she thought.

He smiled, and it was a gloating smile. "Not until December. She comes back for Christmas."

"What about food?" Cara asked.

"There's plenty of tins, I'll fetch some fresh food tomorrow morning. We need to keep you well fed."

Cara shuddered and tried to hide it from him. If he went out the next day it would be her chance to escape. "Would you mind if I went to lie down?" she asked. "I do get so exhausted." If she pretended to sleep at least she wouldn't have to interact with him.

"Of course, let me show you to the bedroom." He led her up a narrow staircase into a room with a double bed. It was made up.

Cara glanced at the small window thinking she could probably squeeze through but noticed to her dismay that the drop was considerable and a stony driveway lay below. A bad fall might cause her to miscarry or twist an ankle and prevent her from running away. She already loved this baby just as she still loved Matt. Even though he was never going to know about it she would never risk the safety of their child.

Unless she did something like make a rope of torn sheets, which she had only ever read about in books, it wasn't going to be a safe exit.

For now she was stuck here. Unless Declan went out again in the car she was going to have to wait it out until morning.

There was still no sign of Cara the next morning. No answerphone message, no note, nothing.

Fiona and Ann tried all her friends again including Declan, where there was still no response. "We'll try his office later," Fiona said. "Maybe he's staying with that awful secretary of his."

"What about that couple she visited a few weeks ago? The ones she met in Sri Lanka. In Surrey, I think she said it was. Did she leave their number?"

They searched Cara's room and found the letter from Evelyn Hillier in a pile on her desk. A quick call from Ann was enough to establish that they hadn't heard from her either.

"Of course they're now worried like we are. When she does show up we'll have to call all these people again and let them know she's OK."

They were still hoping Cara might just walk in the door but as time went on it seemed increasingly unlikely. It didn't look as though she had planned to be away for the night. Her toothbrush was still in the bathroom, the bag she took on overnight trips was still in her room.

It was time to ring Cara's family. Ann knew them best so she made the call. She got through to Cara's brother Will who had stayed on for the week. "Mum and Dad are out grocery shopping, can I help?"

Ann related everything she could. "It hasn't even been a full day yet, but it's not usual for Cara to be away this long. We were hoping you might have heard from her."

"Not a word. I won't worry my parents yet, but I'll drive up immediately. Do the police know? A recent photo? Yes, I'm sure I can find a couple."

Cara's parents lived about an hour and half away from the university town. While waiting for Will to get there Fiona had called the police again as well as the university, and Ann had made a trip around the neighbourhood in case anyone had seen Cara. It made sense for one of them to stay home in case Cara called. But the phone stayed silent.

Finally Will arrived and it felt like a relief even though it hadn't really advanced things any further. He and Fiona first went to the local police station with the photos of Cara, leaving Ann waiting by the phone, and then they reassembled to decide the next steps.

There was no question of either Ann or Fiona going to class that day, they simply couldn't have concentrated.

They made a list for Will of everyone they could think of that Cara knew and those they had already tried contacting.

"I still haven't got through to Declan," Fiona said. "Even his office number isn't answering. I'm going to go there in person."

There was one person that no one had mentioned. They had all thought about him, separately, but no one liked to raise the subject. Fiona and Ann weren't even sure if Will knew, and vice versa.

Fiona took the initiative. "You must know she's pregnant," she said to Will. It was half a statement, half a question.

"She told us last weekend."

"And who the father is?"

Will's face told her that he did indeed know. "Do you think that's who she's with?"

"Right now it's the only idea I have. I hope she's with him, because I can't think of a better scenario in the circumstances." Fiona didn't articulate what a worse scenario might be. An accident or something even more dreadful were on all their minds. But no one dared to voice their fears.

"I'd better go and see him then. After all, we're soon to be related by blood," Will said.

"I don't think he knows."

"It's about time he did, then."

Fiona and Ann exchanged a glance. They both thought that Cara should have told Matt but she was impossible to persuade. She had been so stubborn in insisting that she didn't want to ruin his life and his girlfriend's happiness.

Maybe she had finally taken their advice, and that's where she was. They all hoped so.

25. Searching

Declan was "not in the office" when Fiona showed up at the insurance company to try to speak with him. She had been there before with Cara a couple of times, when Cara had been meeting Declan and Fiona was shopping, as the office was near the main precinct.

Fiona had already tried going round to Declan's house. No amount of knocking on the door got a response, his car wasn't there, and a neighbour she spoke with said he hadn't seen or heard him come in the previous evening.

It was all starting to add up in a rather horrible way. Even without any knowledge of what Declan or Cara had been up to the previous day, the fact that they were both mysteriously absent was alarming.

The receptionist at Declan's company was a young girl with cheaply streaked hair and long plastic fingernails. Fiona wondered for a moment if she was the infamous Lucinda but her name turned out to be Mandy.

Mandy tried to be evasive for the sake of being difficult as it made her feel important to delay people's requests. She also didn't like Declan and wasn't inclined to help anyone who apparently knew him.

She met her match in Fiona. Within a few minutes, Fiona had wrested the information from her that Declan had not shown up that day despite not calling in sick, nor had he been seen since leaving for a meeting the day before. She also discovered that Lucinda no longer worked there.

"I need to know where she's working now. Plus her home address." Fiona didn't bother to ask, she simply demanded.

"I really shouldn't be giving this out. I don't have permission." Mandy looked nervous.

"This is urgent and I don't want any more of my time wasted." Fiona didn't have to fake impatience, her fears for Cara were growing and the urgency sounded in her voice.

The girl crumbled as Fiona knew she would, and wrote down an address on a post-it note. "But don't say you got it from me."

* * *

Will had no idea where Matt lived but he got hold of a newspaper and figured out that he would be playing a county cricket match in Surrey that day.

Traffic allowing he would get there during the lunch break, and if not there was the afternoon tea break. If he had to stake out the ground until night he would do so. He didn't know or care what reception he would get. He was relying on announcing himself as "Cara's brother" to be enough shock for Matt to agree to see him.

Even if the guy had no intention of seeing his sister ever again, and had merely used her which was what Will currently assumed, he would probably be hoping to avoid exposure. It was Will's only leverage though he hoped to gain access to him without threat.

He found a parking spot by the ground, bought a ticket and made his way in. It felt somewhat absurd to be buying a ticket in the circumstances. He had a very slim hope that perhaps Cara was here, watching the cricket, and he looked out for her just in case.

By the time he was inside play was once again underway so he had to wait until the next break, which was mid-afternoon. Being midweek the ground was fairly empty since only retired people had the leisure to watch most county games.

When the players finally went inside again Will made his way to the pavilion and found some kind of official who referred him to someone else. Despite his intense efforts at persuasion he was met with a brick wall, but by chance one of the county players was walking by and heard him arguing with the staff member and giving the name Matt Curran.

Will did not look like a mad fan, he looked as worried as he felt, and the player didn't care for the staff member who was obstructing him. "Do you need to get a message to Matt?" he asked. "I'm going back there now, I can take it for you."

Stupidly Will hadn't thought to bring pen or paper with him, so he told the player to tell Matt that he was "Cara's brother, and it's urgent."

Her name rang no bells with the player as he wasn't on the national team and had no idea of the gossip in Sri Lanka. He agreed to let Matt know and then all Will could do was wait.

"You can't wait here," the staff member said.

Will simply ignored him.

Within a couple of minutes the door opened again, and he was finally face to face with the man that had likely ruined his sister's life.

He had imagined the cricketer to come across as arrogant and cocky but at first glance Matt looked very normal and civil. He was also much taller and broader than Will had expected, which further discouraged him from indulging his urge to punch him.

Matt dismissed the staff member so they could speak more privately. "It's alright, I can handle this. Just give us five."

Five minutes after ruining his sister's life? Will once again wrestled with his instinct to attack Matt. "I'm Cara's brother," he said. "She's gone missing, we've informed the police, and I wondered if she was with you."

Just the sight of Will unsteadied Matt because he looked so much like Cara. The thought that she was in danger gripped his stomach. But he tried not to show any emotion. "She's not with me. If I hear any thing I'll let you know."

Will felt like he was getting the brush off and it irked him. He played his trump card. "You know she's pregnant?"

"Yes, I did know." Matt feigned indifference although the thought of if was still unbearable.

What the hell? What was this guy, some kind of Lothario? "That's your reaction?"

"It's not mine."

If Will knew how much it cut Matt to say these words he wouldn't have taken a swing at him. Fortunately Matt had the quicker reaction and caught his arm before getting hit.

"Of course it's yours, you bloody idiot," Will said, his voice raising to a shout as he wrestled his arm from Matt's grasp. "What do you think my sister is?"

"Calm down. I'm not trying to duck my responsibilities. But it's her ex-fiancé's, not mine." Matt couldn't believe he was having this bizarre altercation with Cara's brother. What the hell had she been saying to her family?

"Did she tell you that?"

Matt faltered. "No, he did."

"You mean Declan? When did you meet him?"

"Yesterday. I went to see her but he was there, gave me the good news and told me she was too sick to come out."

"He told you it was his?" Will asked.

"Yes. 'We're having a baby' were his exact words."

Will felt chilled. "I can assure you it's not his. I saw her face when she told me about you. She would never lie about something like that."

"Could she have told him it was his to get back with him?" Matt's apprehension was growing as he remembered Declan's slightly menacing demeanour.

"She can't stand him. None of us can."

This was the first decent thing Matt had heard for a while. Then he realised what Will was also saying. If Declan was lying or mistaken, then Cara was pregnant with his child. And she was missing and likely in grave danger.

His world turned. "We've got to find her. I'll come back with you straight away."

"Aren't you needed here?" Will asked.

"There's only a couple of hours left." They were fielding and they could put a substitute in for him with a bit of arm twisting the umpire. After all this was an emergency. Explanations could come later.

* * *

Lucinda, Declan's former secretary and mistress, was now working at another company across town. Fiona made her way there not really knowing what to expect. If Lucinda was back with Declan it would likely be news to her that he was still pestering Cara constantly, and not very pleasant news at that.

Prepared for a hostile reaction, Fiona asked the woman behind the front desk for Lucinda.

"And who's asking?"

"I'm a friend of Declan's," Fiona said, wincing at having to use the phrase.

"I've got nothing to say to you, then. Good day."

The woman who was evidently Lucinda, turned her head back to her screen, dismissing Fiona.

"I need your help. He might be in trouble," Fiona told her.

"I'd be very glad to hear that he was. Now I'm very busy and I'd appreciate it if you could let me get back to my work." She had been filing her nails when Fiona arrived so this was obviously a lie.

"It's not him I'm worried about. It's Cara. His ex-fiancée, remember? Ex thanks to you."

Lucinda looked defensive. "It's not my fault if he preferred me to her. I wasn't the one cheating on anyone. He made all the moves, I'll have you know."

"I'm not having a go. I'm one of her flatmates and I'm actually grateful to you for splitting them up. But he's now gone AWOL and she's been missing all night. We need to find out if he's with her and if so where they might be." Fiona was getting exasperated. She was also mystified as to how anyone - even Declan - could cheat on Cara with such a horrible woman. Lucinda wasn't even particularly pretty or intelligent.

"I don't know why you think I would know. I haven't seen him for weeks. Months even," Lucinda said.

Fiona didn't give up. "When you did know him, were there any places he went? Maybe somewhere he took you other than his house."

"Not really. He took me to his country cottage once but it was a bit of a dump and miles from anywhere so I said I didn't want to go back there again."

A remote country cottage. This was sounding more like it. "Do you remember the address?"

"God no. It was in the middle of nowhere. All fields and farm smells. There wasn't even a nice country pub anywhere around."

It might be listed in the phone directory. Fiona suggested this.

"I shouldn't think so," Lucinda said. "It was his aunt's not his, and there wasn't even a phone there. Or a TV. It was awful."

Fiona wasn't going to get anything more out of the woman so she may as well head back and let the others know. If Cara had ever been to the cottage there was a chance she might have told Ann of its location. Certainly Fiona had never heard of it. Or the police might have some way of finding it.

"Thanks anyway. If you do remember anything, here's my number. It could be really important. We've already got the police involved."

There was a flash of alarm in Lucinda's eyes.

"I can't stand the man but I suppose I've got nothing against her. If anything does come to mind, I'll let you know."

Fiona suspected she was more motivated by the thought of getting Declan arrested than helping Cara, but any help was welcome right now.

26. Rescue

Will rang before leaving Surrey to update them.

"It's looking like it must be Declan. Apparently he was over at your place yesterday and to cut a long story short, he wouldn't let Matt in the door."

"You've seen Matt Curran?" Fiona was on the other end of the line.

"He's here with me now. We're driving back as fast as we can."

"I've got one lead," Fiona told him. "Apparently Declan has access to some cottage in the countryside. Lucinda told me about it but she had no idea where it is. It's within an hour or so drive from town, but she didn't even know the direction. We've told the police but they don't seem to be on high alert because there's no sign of a struggle. As far as they're concerned she probably left of her own free will or whatever."

"Hopefully they can at least find the cottage. Just hang in there, we'll be with you soon."

Will and Matt started the drive in silence but the tension became unbearable. Matt kept remembering how weird Declan had been and it chilled him. He didn't know the guy but he could still tell something really untoward was going on. What if the reason he wouldn't let Matt in the door to see Cara was because...? No, he couldn't even start thinking along those lines. But if he had tried to coerce Cara into something and there had been a struggle...

He kicked himself for not just pushing past him and seeing Cara for himself. He replayed it again and again in his mind. He had to distract himself. "Do you live nearby?" he asked Will.

"No, I work up North," Will told him.

It was hard to hold a conversation given how anxious they both were, except for a few remarks. Matt asked Will what he knew of Declan and if he had been unstable in the past. They both avoided explicitly discussing Cara or Matt's personal life but their mutual fears were obvious.

Will wanted to hate Matt for the injustice he felt that the England cricket captain had done to his sister but he couldn't help liking him. It was clear the other man was incredibly worried about Cara. He obviously had strong feelings for her but he wasn't a man who wore his heart on his sleeve.

Will could admire that. He could see how it would be a necessary skill for sport as well, not showing emotion to your opponents.

They finally got back at the end of the day, there were still a couple of hours left before it got dark. Fiona and Ann had maps spread out over the coffee table. "Lucinda rang back and remembered a few more details about the cottage. Apparently they stopped at a service station just before taking an exit off the motorway. She thinks it was about twenty minutes to half an hour after that. She also remembered going through a ford, not long before they arrived," Fiona told them.

"A ford?"

"She said the stream ran over the road, and she thought it was flooded but Declan said it was always like that. So she must have meant a ford. It's hard to figure out exactly where as you'd need a detailed Ordnance Survey map to get the symbols, but there are a few places where streams look like they cross roads."

"Shouldn't we just give all this to the police?" Will said.

"We have. But we're not convinced they're serious about putting out a proper search yet, so we thought we'd give it a go ourselves. It must be the Weston Bridges service station as that's the only one out of town to the north, towards the countryside.

Then I figured we could find a nearby pub and ask someone about fords in the area. They're pretty rare after all."

It was a plan and it was all they had for now.

They couldn't all go in Will's car as someone needed to stay behind in case Cara or the police phoned. Or Cara got home by herself, but no one really believed that was still a possibility.

Will was determined to drive as it was his car and he wanted to be the one to search for his sister. Fiona knew the area best. Matt insisted on going. "I can hardly stay behind after what you've told me," he said.

They were all a bit in awe of him despite the circumstances so no one argued with him. He was internationally famous, constantly in the papers due to his sporting career and his high profile relationship, and there he was in their flat. It added to the surrealism of it all.

* * *

By the time they had reached the motorway exit and found a country pub to inquire about fords it was getting late. It added to the urgency since finding their way around unlit country roads in the dark would be nearly impossible. Fortunately it was June, just a couple of weeks from the solstice, so they had some daylight left.

They were told about two different fords in the area and the landlord of the pub even had a more detailed map.

The first ford was near a large village after which there was a main road and the urban sprawl started soon after. It didn't seem to be the kind of remote place that Lucinda had remembered.

The second really did look in the middle of nowhere. There was a hamlet of a few houses and a couple of farms. There were also buildings here and there that could have been isolated cottages but the map was a few years old so it was hard to be sure.

"That one burnt down a few years ago," the landlord told them. "Elm farm. Vandals it were."

The good news was that there weren't many roads after the second ford. Once you went through it the road forked but they should have time to check out either direction.

"I hope we're on the right track," Fiona said. "This could be a wild goose chase."

It was better than doing nothing though. They were all fairly certain that Cara was with Declan and unwillingly so.

"Did Lucinda remember anything else?" Will asked as they finally passed the ford.

"Yes, it was down a dirt track, the driveway to the cottage."

This wasn't enormously helpful because most of the lanes leading off the main road, many of which weren't even marked on the map, seemed to be unsurfaced.

With dusk falling they were starting to lose hope as the reality of the roads was far more complex than the map had suggested. Then car headlights appeared ahead of them and a vehicle sped past them, nearly clipping Will's wing mirror in the narrow country lane. Fiona swivelled her head as it passed.

"I swear that's Declan's car. I couldn't see the plate but it's the right colour and model."

"Was Cara in it?" Matt asked, his whole body suddenly tense.

"I couldn't see who was inside it," Fiona said.

There was a brief debate about whether they should pursue him. Both the men wanted to but Fiona was against it. "If she's in there with him and he gets panicked by us following him, he might start driving dangerously. The roads around here are unlit and twisty and it's too much risk. But his car will be easy for the police to trace."

"You think we should keep going?" Matt asked.

"If she's with him it's best the police handle it. If he's left her behind somewhere, this is our chance to find her."

"If he's going in that direction he's probably going out for something, food maybe," Will said. "There's nothing the other way. So the cottage will be in the opposite direction."

They kept driving and after another half mile they came to a track. Hopeful, Will drove down it but it seemed to end up in a field so they had to turn around to the main road.

The next track was a left turn off the road. As they went down it they could see a building in the distance. A small house. Grey stone, narrower and taller than one might expect for a cottage.

"This has to be it," Fiona said. "If he's taken her anywhere, it's here."

* * *

Cara had spent a terrible night and a worse day. Declan hadn't even trusted her not to try and leave in the night so he had actually handcuffed her to the bedrail. She had no idea where he would have got handcuffs and the thought of him driving around with them, planning this, horrified her. He took the key downstairs far out of her reach.

She pleaded with him not to do it, promising that she would stay, but he kept telling her he was trying to keep her safe. "The stairs are very steep. If you sleepwalk in the night you could hurt yourself and the baby," he told her.

Cara had never sleepwalked in her life. Her only one relief was that Declan hadn't tried to force himself upon her yet. She had been terrified of what his plans were in that regard but so far he seemed to be treating her as a sacred vessel, untouchable.

He even slept in the other room which was a huge relief. In the morning he released her so she could go to the bathroom. She had barely slept through fear and discomfort and was so exhausted and nauseous she felt her legs would fail her if she did try to run.

"What would you like for breakfast?" The cheeriness of his voice was eerie, he was acting as though they were on some happy holiday together.

"Just some toast." She couldn't stomach anything but she knew she had to eat something.

There was no bread or milk or anything fresh so Declan got her a cup of water and went out to find a local shop. He handcuffed her again to the bed before he went.

"I don't want you hurting yourself."

He went out and returned about forty minutes later with a shopping bag of food.

There followed a long and awful day where Cara could not keep anything down. She didn't know whether it was fear or the pregnancy or whether she was actually ill with some kind of bug.

She was just sick all day and in absolute despair. By early evening she was begging Declan to take her to a doctor and he promised to do so in the morning. She didn't believe him but she had no choice.

"Is there something I can get you tonight?" he offered.

Cara could only drink water at the cottage because caffeine made her ill which ruled out instant coffee and tea, and milk turned her stomach. She had a brainwave. "Some sort of cold fizzy drink would be great. Maybe if there's a pub nearby we could go together?"

Declan gave a hollow laugh. "You're in no fit state to go out. I'll go and see what I can find."

Being alone was at least better than being with him. She was so weak that he took the risk of leaving her downstairs, on an armchair with a blanket over her, even though there was nowhere to handcuff her. All the windows had anti-theft locks and he had taken the key for those. He also locked the front and rear doors so they couldn't be opened from inside.

"I won't be long. You'll be alright," he told her.

Cara felt huge relief when he was finally gone. Even if she only had half an hour or so it was something. It gave her time to think. He surely couldn't keep her there indefinitely. At some point he must come to his senses and take her home. Unless his madness escalated...

She sat there half in a daze, unable to cry, unable to move from the chair. Then she saw the car lights again, shining through the window and moving over the walls as it swung round in an arc.

There was a loud knocking at the door. "Hello? Is anyone there?"

It wasn't Declan. But she was too far gone to even feel relief or be able to call out.

"Cara, are you in there?"

It was Matt.

27. Reunion

Afterwards it was hard to remember exactly how it all happened. Cara was so overcome that all she could do was call out "help" and the next thing she knew the door was burst open and Matt and her brother Will came falling into the room.

Fiona was there and Cara remembered having her arms around her and being helped up and bundled into the car.

"Let's get you out of here."

She couldn't even remember who said it.

There was some argument as to whether to take her to a hospital or not but she managed to tell them that she just wanted to go home and eventually this was agreed on.

Cara was in the front seat, Will driving again. She had no idea how or why Matt was there. No one asked her any questions which was a blessing as she couldn't face talking. Where was Declan? If he didn't know they had taken her, and he found her gone… she shuddered with fear. The thought of him out there, enraged, was terrifying.

"Should we go to the police first?" Fiona asked.

"It might be wise. Can you handle that, Cara?" It was Will who asked her.

She would manage it somehow. "Yes."

It wasn't too much of an ordeal down at the station. A female officer, who was very sympathetic, was assigned to Cara. Some photos were taken of her wrists which had some bad bruising and injury from the handcuffs. There was also a large bruise on her face where Declan had struck her when he found out about the pregnancy. They asked her various questions and it was all typed up and then she had to read through and sign it.

There was now a warrant out for Declan's arrest and Cara was given some basic safety advice.

She was dying to know how they had found her and why Matt was there, but she was so exhausted that she nearly fell asleep in the car.

"You go straight to bed, we'll all be here all night," Fiona told her. "The doors are all locked, Matt and Will can crash in the living room, there's no way anyone is going to get in let alone get past them."

* * *

Matt had been shocked at how Cara looked when they found her in the cottage. She was incredibly pale and tired and had clearly been through an ordeal. The bruise on her face particularly enraged him. Declan would be lucky if the police found him before Matt and Will did.

Mostly Matt blamed himself. He had had the chance to intervene that day, he should have known something was up, but instead he had left her in the clutches of her deranged ex-fiancé. His pride and knee-jerk reaction once again getting in the way of his common sense and better judgement.

Matt was also frustrated because he was dying to just be with Cara, alone, but he understood the importance of her friends and family right now. He wasn't yet family. Hopefully that would one day change.

He had switched his phone off a few hours ago and had no desire to turn it back on. He knew there would be a dozen or more missed calls and voicemails asking where the hell he was.

Right now his only focus was Cara and sorting out the mess and misunderstanding. Hoping that she would forgive him, if he could ever forgive himself for what he must have put her through.

When Cara awoke in the morning he was there. Matt. She had had the strangest and most awful dreams, but through them a realisation that she was safe again and that Matt was nearby.

"Hello." He was sitting by her bed.

She blushed, thinking how terrible she must look with her hair all over the place and her face bruised.

Matt thought she looked beautiful. Natural and sensual.

"Did you sleep well?" He couldn't think of anything else to say. He had so many things to tell her, but no idea where to begin.

"Yes, and you?"

"As well as can be expected, tucked up on the sofa bed with your brother," he told her.

They looked at one another. Questions were flying through Cara's mind but she didn't dare ask any of them. There was an uneasy silence and she was worried that he must have found out from Will or Fiona and be furious about things. Otherwise why was he here?

It was Matt who broke the ice.

"Are you having my child?"

His tone wasn't accusatory, that was something.

Cara spoke in a rush. "Yes but I'll manage, I don't want to cause problems for you. It was my fault, after all." She was surprised by the hurt in his eyes.

"It's not a fault, it's our baby."

Our baby? Cara didn't know how to respond. She still shrank from the thought of what Miggy's reaction would be, to find out that her fiancé had fathered a child during a holiday fling. Seeing her hesitate, Matt spoke again.

"Cara, if I had known, I would have come to you immediately. When I saw you that night… why didn't you tell me?" He meant outside the nightclub, a few weeks ago when they had shared that stolen kiss.

"I didn't know then," she told him. "Then when I did find out I didn't want to ruin your life. To spoil things for you with your…" she didn't know whether to say "girlfriend" or "fiancée" but both words stuck in her throat.

He half smiled but then grew serious.

"Firstly, regardless of that situation I would have wanted to know and I would have wanted to be there for you." With you, he thought, but didn't say it. "Secondly, all that is no longer happening. I won't bore you with the details but it turned out not to be mine and we are no longer together."

So he was free. Probably the last thing he wanted was to jump into another relationship and have yet another pregnancy complicating his life. "I'm sorry," Cara said.

"What for?"

"For all that happening to you, and then for me complicating everything again."

Matt decided they were getting nowhere and it was time to lay all his cards on the table.

"I haven't wanted to be with Miggy for a long time. From long before I met you in Sri Lanka, if I'm honest. When I landed and got her news I felt like I should do the right thing and stand by her. I felt it was the right thing, anyway. Before that happened I had every intention of coming back here and seeing if you wanted to pick up where we left off."

Though Cara was still pale and tired her face lit up at his words. He didn't think she had ever looked more beautiful. Despite the dark shadows under her eyes and looking as though she hadn't eaten properly in weeks, she was radiant.

"What you said outside the nightclub," he continued, "it goes for me too. It wasn't just a bit of fun, it may have started that way but you became far more than just some girl to me. You made me realise that I was with the wrong person, and that I needed to be with you."

Matt didn't think he had ever spoken about his feelings so candidly before but he couldn't risk losing her again.

He didn't wait for her to reply. Infinitely gently he brushed her hair back from her face and brought his lips down on hers. She melted into him. She also felt the blood rush through her at his touch.

Just being with him was coming home. She had dreamt of this, hoped for it, for so long. His kiss was as she remembered: firm, warm, possessing her. She could already taste the urgency on him. He wasn't the only one who wanted more.

She broke off and looked at him hesitantly. "I need to shower," she told him. "Do you want to…"

"Do I want to join you? What do you think?"

Not caring how scandalised her brother or flatmates might be, or that the shower cubicle was hardly as spacious as the one in the hotel in Sri Lanka, she led him to the bathroom and they stepped under the steaming water together. Matt saw that despite being thinner Cara had a slight, firm swell to her stomach. He ran his hand over it and felt suddenly inflamed with tenderness and lust, knowing that she was carrying his child.

His reaction surprised him because he had felt the opposite with Miggy. He hadn't desired her at all since coming back from Sri Lanka. But maybe that wasn't the pregnancy. Maybe that had been because of her and the fact that he was over her.

They also hadn't slept together since he had got back. Matt calculated it was over three months since he'd had sex which was some realisation. He usually had a pretty high sex drive.

"There hasn't been anyone else since you," he told her.

"Really?" It was Cara's turn to be surprised.

"It just didn't feel right. Now I know why." He brought his mouth down on hers again, his hands roaming all over her body, glorying in her slim curves and the way she arched against him.

Cara was amazed that after all she had been through she had been able to recover so quickly. Also that despite being pregnant her body still reacted like this to him. She felt his muscles and the shape of his shoulders, things she had committed to memory and was now rediscovering.

His tongue entwined with hers, the water of the shower running over their faces, drinking one another in. Somehow he instinctively knew that her breasts were more sensitive than usual and he cupped them gently in his hands as he embraced her.

"Let's go back to your room," he said and they went back there and he laid her down on the bed.

As she lay on her back, naked, he kissed her stomach. She was sexier than ever now she was pregnant, or maybe it was the knowledge that she was completely his now. His child, in the girl he desired more than anything or anyone in the world.

Keeping his passion in check as best he could since his primary urge was to bury himself inside her as quickly as possible, Matt gently parted her legs and put his mouth between them. He wanted to ensure she was completely ready for him, that she wanted him as much as he wanted her.

As his tongue swirled over her, first lightly then firmly, he could tell by her soft moans that she was getting close. He wanted to be inside her when she came so he could feel it around himself.

He slipped a finger inside her, into the hot slick tightness of her. She writhed with pleasure at his touch.

He couldn't delay any longer.

He moved back up over her, moved his knees between her thighs, positioned himself and pushed into her. He had thought he might have to take it slowly but she rose against him, drawing him in. The sensation around him was indescribable.

Matt had forgotten how amazing she felt, how much better than any other woman he had ever been with. Physically they fitted exactly. She surrounded him completely. She was made for him.

Cara felt light headed with happiness, relief and the sensations her body felt under his hands and with his skin pressed against hers.

She had been in a nightmare - long, dark, lonely months and the escalating fear and shock of Declan - and now she was back in a dream. Back in Sri Lanka, just the two of them.

He felt larger than he had before, truly filling her.

"I've never stopped wanting you," he told her. And he showed her just how much. He ground into her, increasing the rhythm as she moved against him, meeting each of his moves.

There was no holding back. There was no need to hold back.

He exploded into her just as she reached her own white hot, spasming peak. His woman, the mother of his child. His once again. He vowed to make love to her every day and never let another man near her again.

28. Making plans

Everyone seemed to be treating her with cotton wool the next day which Cara appreciated but she longed for some normality.

Matt refused to leave her and even wanted to ditch his next county cricket match to stay with her. She couldn't go to his place because finals were just a couple of weeks away.

"I'm not leaving you while that maniac is at large," he told her.

Fiona and Ann had promised to stick to Cara like glue and never let her out of their sight. Will was also reluctant to leave but Cara managed to persuade him she would be fine.

There were a couple more days before Matt had to get back so he suggested they go away for a short break. He liked Cara's friends and felt grateful to them for helping with the rescue, but he wanted to be alone with her. "Just take tomorrow off."

"It's the Queen's birthday in Australia, they get a public holiday," Fiona said. "She's our queen, we should do so as well."

Cara wasn't sure if this excuse would hold water with her tutors, but they were mainly doing revision now anyway and she could study for that anywhere.

"Where shall we go?"

"I'll book us into a quiet hotel. You can study there all you want to." Matt had no intention of letting Cara do any revision once he got her alone.

Before they left the police rang. It was good news: they had apprehended Declan. They needed Cara to go down again for a few formalities.

"I'll drive you down," Will offered. "It's probably best if you stay here," he said to Matt. By some miracle Matt hadn't been recognised at the police station on the previous night. The officers there had either not been cricket fans or had been too preoccupied with other things to notice.

Matt's involvement in something like this would be all over the newspapers immediately and they all wanted to spare him and Cara from that.

Cara was tense with nerves at the thought of having to face Declan again but Will assured her she wouldn't even see him. "He'll be in some kind of cell. He'll probably be held overnight as the courts won't be open until tomorrow. Given the severity of what he's done they're hardly going to release him without bail. But you'll be safely away with Matt so don't worry."

"What about Fiona and Ann?" Cara was worried for her friends' safety.

"I should think he'd have more to fear from them than the other way round. You saw how furious Fiona was. Matt seems a good bloke anyway, you'll be ok with him."

From Will this was high praise. He had always been protective of his younger sister and had loathed Declan.

"You like him, then?" Cara asked.

"If he treats you well, then yes."

* * *

Will had offered to drive them to the hotel as Matt didn't have his car there but Matt ordered a taxi.

"It's miles," Cara protested.

"Then I'll have miles alone with you in a cab," Matt said.

She had been happily surprised with the ease at which they fell back into being together. The length of time they had spent apart, the overwhelmingly difficult things that had happened to both of them, all just melted away.

They did need to talk though. After all they had hardly known each other for very long and now they were going to have a child together.

Matt was looking forward to introducing Cara to his parents. They had been upset and confused when he had told them the truth about Miggy's pregnancy. Now he had something even more confusing but also wonderful to tell them.

Nothing had appeared in the press yet, and that was going to be another issue. It would be hell when all broke loose on Fleet Street. It wasn't a story that would stay discreetly on the back sports pages where Matt usually appeared. This would be national news, splashed across the tabloids, there would likely be media camping outside their doors. More due to Miggy's fame than his, but it made no difference.

It was going to be the scandal of the year, not least because he knew Miggy would embrace it rather than hide, and he was worried about exposing Cara to it.

The hotel was a historic building in a lovely part of the countryside. It was the kind of place where weddings were held but early in the week they would be pretty much undisturbed.

Matt checked them in under Cara's name for privacy's sake. He had booked the largest suite they had available. It had views over rolling hillside down to a river valley below: no cars, no houses, no people.

"It's so beautiful. I keep thinking the ocean should be outside," Cara said. She was only half joking. Being with Matt in a hotel again took her straight back to Sri Lanka.

"Come here." He drew her onto the bed beside him, his arm around her as they lay there together. "There's something I need to ensure you're clear about." He rolled over and looked into her eyes so she knew he was serious.

"Regardless of you being pregnant, I would still want to be with you. I'm not with you because of the pregnancy, and I wouldn't not be with you if you weren't." He saw the relief in her eyes. So she had been worrying about it.

"I'm also very glad about it, I want to get that out of the way as well. I realise we didn't plan it, and you're about to graduate and have plans for your career. I don't want to stand in the way of that and I'll help enable you in any way I can to do whatever you want to do. If you want a nanny from the moment it's born that's fine. I don't want you to feel pressured into anything."

Cara smiled. "I think I'll want to take a bit of time out. My parents have already offered to help so it will be OK." She meant with living expenses and accommodation. She didn't want him to think she planned to leech off him.

"Cara, you are with me now. You are having my baby and I'll support you both. You're not alone in this any more."

She felt her eyes well up because he had brought back what it had been like these past weeks. Having to cope with it all by herself and conceal the details from everyone.

He saw that she was moved and went to kiss her. The taste of her, the feel of her skin, her scent. He got powerfully hard almost instantly.

"Now however I am going to interrupt your plans to study, because I have other plans for you."

His kiss grew more passionate as he moved over her. Cara loved having him above her: his size, his strength.

He unbuttoned her blouse and moved his hands under the fabric, feeling the growing swell of her breasts. It was like unwrapping a present, she was more than perfect with her new curves.

Cara felt her skin sing at his caress. Even when he was gentle with her he was still insistent, still the one in charge.

"The second you graduate you're moving in with me so I can enjoy this every night," he told her. Had honestly never been so in lust with any girl before. He was insatiable for her.

He drew the rest of her clothes off and gloried in her body. Her tan had long faded but her limbs were like silk, the perfect shape, his alone to enjoy.

She was more than responding to him, wresting his own shirt off, unbuckling his belt. He felt himself twitch and throb as her hands slid onto him to release him from his clothes, he nearly came at her touch. It was like being a schoolboy again. He was already ripe to bursting.

"I'm not going to last long," he warned her.

"We have all afternoon and all night, and then all of tomorrow, and then tomorrow night."

She was teasing him but right at that moment he couldn't imagine doing anything for the next forty-eight hours except making love to her.

She opened for him and he drove inside her, feeling her warm, wet heat around him.

He was barely inside her when he totally lost control. He said her name over and over, gripping her to him as his body was racked in a kind of exquisite torture.

"I want you too badly, that's the problem," he said.

Cara was still in ecstasy just from the feel of having him so close. Matt slid his fingers to where he knew she was most sensitive, staying inside her. He pressed and swirled his fingers around, watching her flush and her eyes glaze with the sensation.

He had such command of her body that he brought her to orgasm within a minute, and as she spasmed around him he already felt himself growing hard again. He wondered which of them would face exhaustion first.

* * *

She was so easy to be with. Matt had forgotten how relaxed Cara made him feel, how she took the weight of the world off his shoulders just by being there.

They were still discovering things about one another. Both of them had been guarded to some extent in Sri Lanka as it was only supposed to be temporary.

"Will there really be such a fuss when it all comes out?" she asked him.

"Immense. But we'll get you away somewhere."

He knew that time was running out in terms of keeping it from the media. Miggy had promised to share her plans for that with him but he knew what she was like. She might spot a sudden opportunity and "leak" something.

Either way come the end of August the game would most definitely be up. JJ had promised to manage it so that Matt didn't look like a deserter or humiliated, and Miggy didn't get hung out to dry as a scarlet woman cheating on an England hero.

Then of course there was Cara, and Matt's actual child on the way, though this could possibly be kept under wraps for a few more months. Cara wasn't due until mid-November which bought them time. Matt hoped that the furore over Miggy's baby would render any future events in his personal life less shocking.

Did he want to spend until November sneaking around though? He was proud of Cara, proud of this pregnancy. He wanted to be able to be seen openly with her and stop all the concealment.

Patience. He just needed to take things carefully and follow JJ's lead. After all he was a master of the dark arts of publicity.

That night they made love yet again. The moon was a couple of days past full and it streamed into their room, cold and pure. Gleaming white, different from the golden moon of Sri Lanka.

He was rocking into her tenderly, looking down into her eyes which shone in their strange and beautiful way.

"I love you," he told her.

Cara was overwhelmed. She knew how she felt about Matt, she had known for months, but she had no idea he returned her feelings to the same extent.

She had hoped it might grow over time, but here he was, already saying it.

"I love you too."

His lips met hers and they were one flesh.

29. Graduation

For the next few weeks Cara filled her head with revision for her finals. Beyond that swirled a mix of terror and joy, heightened by the overall stress and adrenaline of exam time.

Joy of course came from now officially being with Matt. He phoned her constantly and sent her flowers. She was also joyful about her pregnancy which was now something to look forward to so much more. She could be open about it, she didn't have to hide who the father was. To her close friends and family, anyway. Wider acquaintances still had no idea that Cara's boyfriend Matt was not just someone she had "met on holiday who works in London" but actually a household name.

Then there was terror. Part of this came from flashes of insecurity about Matt. Cara was still worried that she might not be enough for him. She still compared herself to the glamorous women like Miggy he had dated previously. But her confidence in his love was steadily growing.

Then there was the fear of Declan. She had a restraining order against him but he had got bail, given it was a first offence, and she would have to face him again at his trial. She didn't know if he would come after her again. If he did, and breached the order, he would go straight into custody. But she didn't want to take the risk of that. Instead she had to avoid ever being alone. Matt had given her a phone which she carried everywhere, just in case.

Finally there was the fear of everything hitting the press. For as long as nothing happened it felt like they were in limbo. She wanted it to be over, but she knew as soon as Miggy's baby arrived she would be flung into the centre of it all. Matt had warned her about this. He hoped to protect her as much as possible but she would still probably have her photo all over the newspapers.

JJ had advised them that curiosity would be immense. He was already fielding inquiries from gossip column journalists who detected something was up between Matt and Miggy as they hadn't been photographed together in weeks. Matt had refused to fake an ongoing relationship, mainly out of respect for Cara. She had told him that she didn't mind if it made things easier, but Matt minded. He wanted to run things on his own terms now, not those of Miggy and her publicist.

* * *

July arrived and with it Cara's graduation as well as the Ashes test match series between England and Australia.

England had lost the first two tests but Matt had played valiantly, motivated by the fact that Cara was watching. He had wanted to get her VIP tickets but she preferred to lie low. Instead she sat with the Hilliers. The grounds for the international games were so large and packed with spectators that she managed to avoid being seen by the other players. Chris knew about her of course, she had met him several times now through Matt and they were already becoming firm friends.

"Such an astonishing turn of events," Evelyn Hillier remarked, not for the first time. "But I did feel, my dear, when you stayed with us that the situation was not yet played out." She had also urged Cara to come and stay again with them before the birth.

Peter Hillier was even more complimentary about Matt's playing in Cara's presence, which she found nice but embarrassing.

Matt managed to make it to her graduation between matches. He had met her parents who liked him very much, all the more so due to his role in helping rescue Cara from Declan.

Fiona took the lead and introduced Matt as her cousin to anyone who asked, and then had to field endless requests for test match tickets from their university friends. Both she had Cara had graduated with high honours and were in a buoyant mood.

"I feel enormous," Cara said.

"Just let the gown flap in front of you, it hides it beautifully," Fiona said.

Stepping back down from the platform holding her degree, Cara caught Matt's eye as she returned to her seat and was moved by the pride she saw there. He wanted her to succeed and be her own person.

* * *

August came. Miggy's baby, a boy, arrived two weeks early and Matt escaped to France with Cara for a short break to avoid the worst of the headlines. By now there had been several leaks about his and Miggy's "estrangement" in the gossip columns so his absence didn't come as the shock it might have otherwise.

True to form, Miggy managed to reel out some dashing South American model who was posing as the father. He was so meltingly handsome in a dark-eyed, Latin way and they looked so glamorous together in photos that it helped with any media disappointment over his obscurity.

"Miggy's Latin lover revealed as baby daddy!" "Miggy and Matt split as England slumps again".

Miggy couldn't bring out the actual father, the Peruvian photographer, since he was married which would have turned it into even more of a fiasco.

She gushed at length at how blissfully happy she was with Roberto and was charmingly self-deprecating about her "foolish mistake" in the timing. She also made a few kind and tactful hints about how Matt had already found "great happiness" elsewhere, leaving the press desperately trying to track down him and his "mystery woman" as Cara was now described.

Frustrated by his escaping their grasp, there were some rather mean spirited articles linking England's poor performance to supposed turmoil in Matt's personal life, even though he had personally played exceptionally well. Fortunately most of the cricket writers liked him and were fairly loyal in their own commentary.

Cara, lying in a field fragrant with meadow flowers deep in rural France, was happily unaware of everything. There was a good bit of time between the third and fourth tests so it was the ideal time for a break, even if it meant neglecting a few of his captaincy duties.

The smell of the long grasses, the heat. The sun on her face and the silence. Just the noises of nature. They seemed to be miles from anywhere.

She plucked a brilliant red flower growing just nearby and played with its delicate petals. "Poppy would be a sweet name, if it's a girl," she said. They were leaving the gender as a surprise.

Matt felt his heart turn over. He was sure he had never mentioned his own liking for the name as they hadn't even discussed names yet. He would have been totally happy for Cara to choose whatever she liked.

"Do you think it's a girl?" he asked her.

"I don't know. Sometimes, when I dream of it. But the other night I dreamt it was a rabbit so you probably shouldn't rely too much on my intuition."

Matt remembered something. He had been waiting for the right moment and there could be no time more perfect than this.

He brought out a box from his pocket. He had been carrying it around for so long he almost forgot it was there.

"This is for you."

Cara opened it and couldn't speak for a moment. It was the largest and most beautiful sapphire she had ever seen, set into a platinum band with two brilliant diamonds on either side. It was clearly an heirloom and without doubt the most valuable piece of jewellery she had ever held.

Matt reached for her hand to slip it on but she bit her lip, looking troubled.

"Is something wrong?"

"It's just that, we hadn't actually discussed…" she was embarrassed to put it into words.

Matt felt like an idiot. "I haven't even asked you to marry me, have I?"

"Not exactly."

He rolled over so he was on one knee, above her as she was lying on the ground. He looked deep into her eyes, thinking once again how incredibly lovely she was and how lucky he was to have found her. She had better say yes.

"Will you marry me? I love you and I want you always, and I have never been so happy as you have made me."

Once again Cara couldn't speak for a moment. She managed to say yes and he put the ring on her finger and kissed her as he did so. She would forever remember the sensation of the ring being slipped on her hand with his lips joining hers.

It felt strangely sacred, as though they were somehow already married in nature, blessed by the wind and the trees and the flowers.

"Believe it or not, it's actually a Sri Lankan stone. My great-grandfather got it for my great-grandmother over half a century ago," he told her. "I didn't even know my mother had it as she wears a ring from my father's side the family."

His mother had deliberately not produced it on his supposed engagement to Miggy, not that he had ever actually asked Miggy to marry him.

It was a strange coincidence, the origin of the ring, given where they had met. "It matches your eyes," he told her.

He caressed her stomach. He loved the shape of it, the firm, growing roundness of it. Despite the fact they were in the open air he wanted her urgently. They were hidden by the high grasses and there was no one in sight.

He slipped his hand under her sundress. "Do you want me?" he asked.

"Always." Cara had been both surprised and delighted that he still wanted her so much despite the changed shape of her body. She had felt self-conscious about it at first but he made her feel beautiful and desirable with his attentions to her, and the obvious reaction she aroused in him.

Gently, because they had all the time in the world, he took her in his arms and let her know just how much she meant to him. For always.

Epilogue

There the honeysuckle blooming,
Reddens the capricious wave;
Richer sweets—the air perfuming,
Spicy Ceylon never gave.

An Evening Prospect
Ann Eliza Bleecker

The Cotswolds, ten years later

The dappled shade under the old apple tree was a comfortable place to study while the children played on the lawn. Poppy and her brother Finn were already keen cricketers and little Rose, a few years younger, was trying hard to keep up.

Cara was hoping she would manage to finish the final draft of her PhD thesis in time. She rested her hands on her stomach, so big and round now that she was sure it must arrive any day now.

Across the lawn the Cotswold stone of their ancient farmhouse glowed golden in the sun. Upstairs she still had to finish preparing the nursery. Thank goodness these old houses had plenty of bedrooms.

She and Matt hadn't planned this pregnancy so most baby things had been given away after Rose no longer needed them. Three children had seemed the perfect family size for them: trust Fate to have another blessing in store. As well as other surprises.

Matt had retired from cricket shortly before Rose's birth to become a writer, hoping it would give him more time at home with Cara and his young family. But success saw him constantly dragged onto book tours and celebrity appearances by his more commercially minded agent. He'd also been in demand as a cricket commentator.

One of the reasons Cara had returned to academia was so that she had more freedom to travel with her husband. Sometimes the children travelled with them, at other times they stayed with their adoring grandparents.

It was an idyllic life. Some days she had to pinch herself to believe things could really be so perfect. Just one thing niggled at her. It was something she needed to tell Matt but he was already concerned about how they would manage a fourth child. Rose started school in the autumn and they had imagined getting some more time to themselves.

It was the one thing Matt regretted: that he hadn't been able to have Cara to himself for at least the first couple of years of their marriage. Not that Poppy hadn't been the light of his life from the moment she came red-faced and screaming into the world, but he treasured the time he did get alone with Cara.

"Daddy!" There were wails of delight from the children as Matt arrived home. Bat, ball and stumps were cast aside as three small bodies flung themselves at him.

Cara felt her heart flutter as she watched, just as it had when she first met him. Despite retiring from professional cricket he had maintained the lean, muscular body of an athlete.

Matt kissed the children and shook them off as he approached Cara. He greeted her gently, always concerned how fragile she might be when pregnant. No matter how much Cara reassured him she was as strong and capable as ever he had a tendency to treat her like rare porcelain.

"I thought we might go and visit your parents this weekend. We can go and visit that artisan woodwork place in the village and see if there are any cots," Matt said.

"About that..." Cara was cut short by a sudden twinge.

Matt was instantly concerned. "Are you alright?"

She was fine. It was just one of those things that happened when your stomach had turned into a watermelon.

Matt loved how Cara looked when she was carrying his child. She was so rounded and full and glowing, and yet somehow she seemed more slim and delicate than ever behind the pregnancy.

"If you're feeling tired we could go and lie down?" he suggested, having no intention of letting her have any rest. For now, anyway. They currently had a housekeeper-come-nanny, a kind elderly woman from the village, who helped supervise the children. Matt had insisted on it so he could at least enjoy some of Cara's undivided attention.

Cara smiled. She knew exactly what he wanted. The thought of being in his arms, alone with him, was as appealing as ever.

* * *

The sun was setting, streaming red gold through the open window and carrying the fragrance of the evening garden with it. Cara lay back on the pillows, her body warm and sated, while Matt showered. He came out, drying himself with a towel. The sunset gilded him as he stood before her.

She was moved by the love and desire she saw in his eyes. It seemed to stream from him, warming her as the fading sunlight did.

"I've got a surprise," he told her.

Cara had been about to tell him something but she let him go first. "A nice surprise?"

"Next weekend I've booked for us to go away. The Hatherley Manor hotel. Without the kids, a last break together before the new one arrives."

Hatherley Manor was the first hotel they had stayed at together, at least in England. It was where Matt had taken Cara all those years ago to get away from all the drama with her former boyfriend. It seemed so long ago now.

Over the years they had stayed at the hotel on several occasions and it held very special memories for them. As did the hotel in Sri Lanka, where they had also returned a couple of times with the children.

"That would be lovely, assuming we don't run out of time," Cara said.

Matt came and lay next to her, putting his hand on her stomach. "You'll just have to tell him or her to wait."

Him or her. Cara knew the answer to this, but she hadn't told Matt. She knew she needed to, particularly if they were about to go and shop for nursery furniture.

"Besides, you've got nearly five weeks to go. All of the others came late."

Cara had a feeling this time was going to be less prolonged. She silently willed herself to keep going as long as possible.

* * *

Of course it would be at the hotel in the middle of the night that Cara was woken by a familiar pang. A painful tightening across her stomach that she knew would repeat and grow in frequency and intensity.

They didn't have much time.

She was ready, prepared mentally anyway. She had worked every minute possible the previous week and finally sent her thesis off for submission. Her supervisor had encouraged her to take her time, given her condition, but Cara knew that after the birth there would be no time at all for ages. She had done all the work and she didn't want to delay any longer. It had already been nearly four years.

She nudged Matt awake. "It's on the way."

"What?" He was confused, foggy with sleep.

"The... baby. On the way."

He swore and leapt out of bed. Called reception. Ordered an ambulance. Carried Cara down the stairs as there wasn't a lift in such an old building. She told him she could managed her own way down but he wouldn't even let her stand by herself.

She loved him for it, even if he was a bit over-protective.

Matt had been there at the birth of all their children and he wasn't about to miss this one. Particularly as they had both vowed it would definitely be their last.

Cara was rushed into a birthing suite. It seemed to happen more quickly every time, and for this one they had only just made it. Although it was a few weeks early the doctors weren't too worried.

She was already in active labour and within just half an hour Matt held his fourth child and second son in his arms.

"I guessed it would be a boy. You alternate," he told her.

Cara only smiled, exhausted, and then she was wracked with another painful contraction.

Matt was still studying the face of the tiny new arrival he was holding when suddenly there was another flurry of activity and the cry of a baby. Except not the one he was holding.

"And a daughter, Mr and Mrs Curran," the midwife said.

Twins?

"Did you know?" he asked Cara.

Cara looked anxious. "Yes. I kept meaning to tell you but it never seemed to be the right moment. I didn't find out until really late. I was going to tell you at the hotel, but..."

Matt laughed. "You were worried I couldn't cope with two more?"

"You did seem a bit overwhelmed with a fourth. I thought a fifth might be pushing it." She was joking, but she had been genuinely anxious. Which looking at him now, absolutely overcome as he was with pride and adoration for the tiny newborn pair, was absurd. She blamed it on pregnancy hormones.

"We'd better ring your parents then. They can double the nursery order." He was absolutely delighted by the surprise. One of each. It was the perfect way to complete their family. The children would be thrilled as well with their new siblings.

"Have you chosen the babies' names?" a nurse asked him.

Had they? Matt had thought they had. It had been so simple, Kit for a boy and Kitty for a girl. They could hardly use the same name twice.

"Any ideas?" he asked Cara.

"This is Kit, of course." He always had been. She had always known in her heart of hearts that Kit would be a little boy. "Then we should probably have another flower name. Do you like Lily?"

Matt liked it.

"It's the national flower of Sri Lanka," she told him. "The blue star water lily, I looked it up. It seemed to fit."

Now Matt loved it. "Lily it is." He picked up his fifth and final child and kissed her forehead. Their little water lily. She had sapphire blue eyes like her mother, like the precious stone that Cara wore on her finger.

He looked at his wife and felt an intense rush of love. They were a team. She understood him better than anyone else ever had. She was, quite simply, the love of his life. His perfect match.

About Noël Cades

Noël Cades is a British writer who currently lives in Sydney, Australia. A fan of romance from historic to erotic, some of Noël's favourite authors include Jilly Cooper, Jackie Collins, Elizabeth Rolls and Victoria Holt.

Noël is always delighted to hear from other fans, readers and writers of romance.

You can contact Noël at noelcades@gmail.com

Noël's website is at http://www.noelcades.com

Visit Noël's blog to sign up for exclusive news and the chance to receive new free book giveaways.

Excerpts from Summer's Edge by Noël Cades

Alice remained silent throughout this. She was still feeling disappointed and uncertain. She tried to tell herself it was for the best. Really, she should be grateful that he had just decided to move past it.

But she still felt embarrassed. She picked at the grass next to her, pulling off a small flower, avoiding looking at the play.

Then a shadow fell over them. She looked up.

It was Mr Walker.

"I want a word with you. In the pavilion, now," he ordered her. His eyes pierced into hers and he looked furious.

Numb, she obeyed, walking ahead of him.

Inside it was empty and he closed the door behind them and turned to her.

"What the fuck do you think you're playing at?"

He was absolutely incensed. He stood there, suddenly the adult, the authority, not just some guy she had kissed in a pub.

Someone she had compromised. Alice couldn't think of anything to say.

She stood there in front of him. His scent of faint cologne and sun-warmed skin was disturbingly familiar to her, mingling with the dusty wood and sports equipment smell of the pavilion.

"Did you know who I was?" he asked.

"Yes." There didn't seem to be any point in lying.

He glared at her and she looked back at him. His eyes pierced into her, their light grey-blue contrasting with his tanned complexion. He was one of the most devastatingly attractive men she had ever seen. All the more so now as his anger turned his face into carved steel.

As terrified and awkward as Alice felt, she also felt slightly defiant. After all she hadn't done anything wrong or illegal.

Then suddenly he grasped her by the shoulders and brought his mouth down on hers, hard. Surprised, she initially squirmed to escape his grasp then yielded as her forced his tongue into her mouth. His lips were bruising hers, he was almost biting her yet she wanted more.

Her hands, which had pushed against his chest to try and get away, went round his neck and she arched against him.

He was trying to hurt her, devour her. Punish her. All at once. But he wanted her too. She could taste his need, raw and urgent. Feel the hotness of his breath as he nearly suffocated her with his kiss.

His mouth left hers and moved to her neck, half embracing, half biting it. She tasted blood on her lip where he had crushed it with his own. He was gripping her hard and she clung to him. She didn't even care that he was hurting her.

He could have ripped all her clothes off right there and forced himself upon her. She had never wanted anyone so much.

Then just as suddenly he thrust her away from him. He swore under his breath as he tried to recover himself.

"Is that what you wanted?"

"No... yes... I mean..." Alice had no idea what to say. She was shaken and half in misery, half in ecstasy.

His face was like granite, its angles unyielding.

"Get out and don't come back here again. Stay out of my way," he said.

* * *

Alice tried to enjoy herself at the barbecue but she couldn't relax with Mr Walker just metres away, deliberately avoiding her. She had no appetite but knew she needed to eat something to avoid getting completely drunk on an empty stomach.

Graeme was good company and buoyed up by misery, alcohol and perhaps a desire to make a point to Mr Walker she flirted with him a bit. He was the kind of guy you could flirt with without it meaning much. Besides she knew he preferred Jules. She also noticed that Mr Walker's gaze was frequently on her and he didn't look happy about her flirting with Graeme. Or she hoped that was why he looked annoyed.

As the beer went down the revelry increased and someone accidentally knocked a glass full of beer over Alice. It went all over her top.

Feeling as though nothing much more could go wrong with the day she found her way to the kitchen and tried to sponge out the worst at the sink. If the beer dried on it, it would smell awful and probably stain the fabric. Hopefully even though she was getting her top even more wet it would dry quickly in the sun.

As she was finishing getting the worst off someone else came into the kitchen. She knew even before she turned that it was Mr Walker. He looked angry.

"Did you come here deliberately?" he asked.

She faced him. "I came here with Becky. I didn't know you'd be here. Or care," she added.

"What have you done to your shirt?"

"Someone spilt beer on it. I was washing it off."

"You can't go back out like that. You look like a wet t-shirt competition," he told her.

Alice looked down and went red. The wet fabric had gone transparent and soaked through her bra too.

Without a word Mr Walker pulled off his own shirt and handed it to her. He wore nothing under it. Alice was transfixed by his physique. His arms rippled with muscle and his flat, hard chest was tanned a deep gold. He was far fitter than she expected a cricketer to be, really powerful looking.

"Put this on."

The shirt was white cotton and warm from his body. She held it. It smelt of him. She wanted to envelop herself in it but she didn't follow his order.

"You want me to walk out of here wearing your shirt with you following me, topless?" she asked him.

He was silent for a moment, glaring at her. She was right, it would have exactly the opposite effect he intended. The situation was bad enough as it was.

"I don't want them gawping at you."

Alice's stomach gave a secret flip. Possessive and protective. He clearly didn't feel as neutrally towards her as he wanted to.

"The sun will dry it. I'll cross my arms." As she said this, she deliberately left her arms uncrossed and put her shoulders back slightly.

It had the desired effect. He was momentarily transfixed.

"Jesus Christ."

Alice took charge of the situation. "You should put this back on." Instead of just handing it to him she went to put it over his head meaning her arms were raised and her body was nearly against his. He was still for a second before taking a step backwards. A muscle clenched in his jaw.

"Just give me the shirt." She did so and he put it back on.

Then they both stood there. The tension was unbearable. She knew he wanted her and was fighting against it with every fibre of his being.

She broke the ice. "I am sorry you know. We were all just having fun the other night and I just didn't think about the implications."

"You were just messing around with me because I'm employed at your school?"

"God no, that wasn't why." Alice couldn't believe he thought this. Surely he'd realised how much she also wanted him to kiss her that night?

"So even if I hadn't been, you would have still put on your little act?" he asked.

What act? "I wasn't acting, I genuinely..."

"You wanted it too?"

"Yes." It was barely a whisper.

For a moment she thought he was going to kiss her again. He was wavering. Then he stood straighter. "I'm way too old for you, Alice, and I work at your school. Get back outside."

Find out what happens between Alice and Mr Walker in Noël Cades' thrilling taboo student-teacher romance, Summer's Edge.

www.ingramcontent.com/pod-product-compliance
Lightning Source LLC
Chambersburg PA
CBHW020959180626
46814CB00003B/1176